KT-220-102

ROSE
RAVENTHORPE
INVESTIGATES
HOUNDS AND HAUNTINGS

Janine Beacham

A former journalist, Janine Beacham has written all her life. She has always loved fairy tales and fantasy, and as a child would make up games for her friends to play at school. Janine once entered a competition where the prize was a real-life butler – which partly inspired the secret society of butlers in the *Rose Raventhorpe Investigates* series. Janine lives in Western Australia with her family.

ALSO BY JANINE BEACHAM

Rose Raventhorpe Investigates
Black Cats and Butlers

Rose Raventhorpe Investigates
Rubies and Runaways

JANINE BEACHAM

LITTLE, BROWN BOOKS FOR YOUNG READERS
www.lbkids.co.uk

LITTLE, BROWN BOOKS FOR YOUNG READERS

First published in Great Britain in 2018 by Hodder and Stoughton

3 5 7 9 10 8 6 4

A CIP catalogue record for this book is available from the British Library.

ISBN 978 1 5102 0132 3

Printed and bound in Great Britain by Clays Ltd, Elcograf S.p.A.

The paper and board used in this book are made from wood from responsible sources.

Little, Brown Books for Young Readers
An imprint of Hachette Children's Group
Part of Hodder and Stoughton
Carmelite House
50 Victoria Embankment
London EC4Y 0DZ

An Hachette UK Company
www.hachette.co.uk

www.hachettechildrens.co.uk

For Dad

For Dad

Prologue

A moonless night was a blessing for a thief.

And the Shudders was a blessing for a pickpocket. By day, the area was a charming shopping district, with cobblestones and rickety overhanging buildings. It bustled with carriages, teashops and gossip. But by night it changed personality. The crooked alleys – skitterways, they were called – turned as cold and narrow as a judge's smile. They belonged to stray cats and dogs, tipsy tavern-goers and people like Moll the Pocket.

A barefoot young woman with a cheeky smile, Moll the Pocket knew her way blindfold around Yorke's skitterways. When drunken men staggered down the narrow streets, Moll was good at pretending to help them. They only noticed her smile, not their purses and watches disappearing.

But pickings were lean tonight. Moll leaned against a window in a skitterway called Mad Meg Lane, shivering in the cold. Hopefully a victim would appear soon. Moll needed money if she was to make rent-day.

She peered into the shadows. A rat scuttled past, but there was no sign of anyone in the distance. Then, out of the foggy darkness, two red, glowing flames appeared.

Moll thought at first it was a man's pipe, but she'd never seen fire that red. She twitched her scrap of a shawl closer. The flames were at the height of her chest. And moving slowly towards her. They swayed a little. That was – odd. She blinked hard. Were there footsteps, and a figure beside them? It was too dark to be sure.

The lights flickered, still that unnaturally bright red. Nearer now, only ten feet away. Moll thought she could see a shape and hear footfalls, but it was hard to tell in the dark. She swallowed, taking a step back. 'Hello,' she said in a voice that was meant to sound cheery. It came out in a croak.

No reply. Still the lights danced. Like eyes, Moll thought. Demon eyes. She thought of the whispered stories she'd heard. Uncanny cat statues come to life. Nonsense of course, but still—

A deep growl sounded in the skitterway, coming from the same place as the eyes. Moll jumped. Her skin prickled. She spun on her heel, ready to bolt.

A cat leapt lightly over a rooftop. The growling grew louder. The eyes disappeared. Something hit Moll in the back, sending her flat on her face. Winded and scared, she lay on the cold cobblestones and wheezed for breath. Her back was in agony, but she forced herself to roll sideways. She struggled up on one knee. She wasn't going down without a fight. She sensed movement behind her and launched herself at the figure.

Then came another blow, this time to the head.

Moll gasped, seeing stars. Rage filled her. No bully took on Moll the Pocket! She shrieked her rage, readied her fists, and hurled herself at her attacker.

In the distance, children sang.

Lurking in the dead of night
Hell-hound Barghest shuns the light.
Sharp of fang and red of eye
He will stalk you till you die.

Chapter 1

Raven and Raventhorpe

Rose Raventhorpe and her friend Orpheus Raven were duelling on the city wall.

It was dawn, and the city was shrouded in chilly, clammy mist from the surrounding moors. Smoke curled from chimneys as their blades clashed. Rose wore white satin frills and a determined expression, while Orpheus cut a dash in a tricorn hat and tailcoat. The son of an English sailor and an Indian mother, Orpheus had catlike balance and quick reflexes learned from months at sea. As the daughter of Lord and Lady Raventhorpe, and a secret guardian of Yorke, Rose could fight like her honour was at stake. This morning, however, Orpheus disarmed her three times in a row.

'What's the matter with you?' he demanded, rubbing at the back of his neck and picking up Rose's weapon. 'Yesterday you could have beaten me on a rooftop with your eyes closed.'

'I don't know!' Rose snapped. Her hazel eyes clouded with anxiety. 'Something's off, something's wrong. Even the walls don't feel right under my feet.' *It's ridiculous,* she told herself. *I've seen dead bodies. I've caught murderers. I've always felt safe up here, always. But not today. Why not?*

Orpheus pushed back his tricorn hat. 'It's because of that woman in the Shudders, isn't it? The attack last night. Look, it's awful that some dog got loose and killed her, but you can't blame yourself. We Guardians can't protect everyone.'

'I know,' said Rose, taking the weapon from her

friend, and perching on the wall. 'But I can't stop thinking about it. Heddsworth learned about it from the butcher's boy this morning. The poor boy found the victim himself. She was a pickpocket named Moll, and her injuries were terrible – she was covered in claw marks, deep scratches, like those from a wolf. We need to find that beast before it hurts anyone else.'

Orpheus shivered and sat down next to her. 'Sounds like the dog they had at the orphanage,' he said. 'That thing gave me nightmares.'

Rose fiddled with her cameo necklace. 'The butcher's boy told Heddsworth that a lantern-lighter saw eyes in the dark last night. And a hansom cab-driver saw a huge shadow near Tatterlace Green.'

Orpheus shrugged. 'A dog that big shouldn't be hard to trace. I'll ask the butlers at Silvercrest Hall to help.'

Orpheus and his sister Inaaya lived at the Silvercrest Hall Academy for butlers, which housed some extraordinary staff and students. Rose had met them while investigating a murder the previous year. Silvercrest Hall butlers learned the usual tasks of serving tea and running a household, but few people knew they also learned the art of duelling. After their training at the Hall, most of the butlers went to work in grand households, but in secret they acted as the Guardians of Yorke, fighting criminals and protecting the city from threat. Orpheus and Inaaya were enjoying their life at the Hall, especially as Inaaya was allowed to jump on her bed and have pillow fights with her brother. The staff didn't mind – it taught the butlers how to clean up after children.

'We'd better use the Stairs Below when we go about Yorke,' Rose decided. 'Just while the dog is uncaught. Make sure you have your Infinity Key with you.'

'Always,' said Orpheus, patting the key on its chain under his shirt. An Infinity Key could open all the doors in Yorke that led to the Stairs Below.

'I'm a Guardian now, like the cats.' He nodded towards the nearby rooftops. The black cat statues of Yorke were visible all over the city. They too were Yorke's guardians in a way few people would believe. Rose had seen them turn into moving creatures who could attack an enemy with the fury of a thunderstorm, and call snow out of the sky. Her own cat, Watchful, shared their talents.

'We need more fencing practice too,' Rose added. 'You have to learn to keep your guard up.'

'Well, you need to work on your balance.'

'Both of you could use some practice,' said another voice.

Rose and Orpheus nearly toppled off the wall. Heddsworth, Rose's butler, had climbed up to sit beside them.

'How did you get here?' spluttered Rose.

Heddsworth dusted off his pinstriped trousers. 'Just because I am considerably older than you does not mean I lack agility, Miss Raventhorpe.'

'I know you're agile,' protested Rose. 'You're

a brilliant swordfighter! I just didn't know you'd followed us.'

'Really, Miss Raventhorpe. You will have to improve your stealth skills if you want to sneak past a Guardian.'

Orpheus grinned. Heddsworth adjusted the rapier he carried under his coat. He gazed at the view of the fog-ridden city.

'A sad morning,' he remarked. 'That poor woman. People are going to be frightened. Particularly as the incident happened in Mad Meg Lane.'

Rose frowned at him, pushing back her dark hair. 'What do you mean?'

'There's a story that the Barghest, the nightmare hound, haunts that lane. An old beggar-woman called Mad Meg was killed there, a hundred years ago. Some stories claim that she was a witch, and raised the Barghest herself. I dare say that Mad Meg was a poor homeless creature who had lost her wits. No more witch than I am.'

'Can we stop talking about nightmare dogs?' Orpheus shivered again.

'It is only a story,' said Heddsworth reassuringly. 'The Barghest is a legend. But the woman's death last night was all too real. We should visit the skitterway immediately and look for clues into the whereabouts of the creature that attacked her. We cannot have it running wild and harming anyone else.'

'We should,' agreed Rose. 'Father would want us to help in his absence.' She turned in explanation to Orpheus. 'He left a few days ago, off again on his ambassador work. Knowing Father, he took a steamer, and a train, and an elephant—'

'You've been reading *Around the World in Eighty Days*, haven't you, Miss Raventhorpe?' said Heddsworth. 'You were supposed to return that book to me once you finished it.'

'I'm rereading it,' said Rose. 'I'm in love with Phileas Fogg.'

'Well, I'm in love with Aouda, so please give it back.'

Orpheus laughed. 'Are you going to get married one day, Heddsworth?'

'Difficult to find a lady to live up to those in literature,' said Heddsworth. 'I rather took to Elizabeth Bennet in that novel *Pride and Prejudice.* Lively, sportive, loves to laugh.'

'You could advertise in the newspapers,' said Rose. '*Seeking a Miss Bennet.*'

'Alas, I do not own a grand estate. I fear that would disqualify me.'

Red and gold lights crowned the horizon. The sunrise kept them quiet for a while. The towers of the great cathedral were inky black against the clouds, and the cat statues of Yorke perched on roofs in perfect silhouettes. Rose smelled smoke from the chimneys and heathery wind off the moors. She sighed with pleasure. Yorke was her home, and she would do whatever it took to defend it.

'Well, we got to enjoy a beautiful sight,' said Heddsworth at last. 'But I need to return home and prepare the breakfast table. Mrs Standish has made her famous marmalade. Orpheus can return to the Hall and inform Miss Regemont about developments. I dare say Bronson and Mr Malone will want to help too. They can meet us at the Shudders after breakfast.'

'Excellent,' said Rose, pleased at both the idea of action and seeing her friends. Miss Regemont was the head of the Hall, and female butler Bronson and secretary Charlie Malone were Heddsworth's best friends. 'Mother won't mind. I'll tell her I'm shopping. She's planning a trip to London, and packing is taking her mind off me.'

'I know all about the packing,' said Heddsworth ruefully. 'Seven trunks and five hatboxes so far. I doubt she would notice if we had a swordfight in front of her.'

'She did say she was worried about Father being abroad,' said Rose, trying to be fair. 'She thinks he'll be stampeded by an elephant.' Personally, Rose thought any elephant foolish enough to do that would be stampeded by her mother. Lady Constance was a society beauty, but she was also steel in a corset.

'Off we go then,' said Heddsworth. 'If we are going to deal with murderous dogs, we should at least have a cup of tea first.'

After breakfast, Rose and Heddsworth took the Raventhorpe carriage to the Shudders. As they alighted from the vehicle, Rose spotted a crudely written placard on a wall:

BEWARE!!

A DEADLY BEAST LURKS IN THIS CITY

WOMAN SAVAGED!!!

'It's good to see no one is panicking,' said Heddsworth drily.

Some passers-by read the notice with puzzled expressions. A few looked alarmed. Several children whispered gory details to each other.

Rose paused to talk to them. 'Did you see anything after the attack?'

'Nay, but we know about it,' one boy boasted. 'A vicious beastie, what ate the woman whole.'

'No, it bit her legs off first,' said another child.

'Did not.'

'Did too.'

Rose was glad to see Orpheus arrive with her butler friends. All of them inspected the placard.

'Now, who do you suppose put that sign up?' wondered Bronson, the sole female butler. She gripped the hilt of her rapier in its special coat pocket. 'A reporter? One of those professional scaremongers?'

'They'd love a story like this,' agreed Charlie Malone. A golden-haired butler-turned-secretary, he had a permanent limp from a fencing injury. 'An excuse for big headlines and terrible punctuation.'

'We must find the dog before there is another attack,' declared Miss Regemont. The imposing head of Silvercrest Hall Academy for Butlers, she and her staff – including Bronson and occasionally Heddsworth – taught students the skills of buttling and ran its secret society of Guardians. She had a steel-grey pompadour hairstyle and looked born to wear crimson velvet. 'It is our duty as Yorke's Guardians. We must find the dog that caused the tragedy. Let us visit the scene, however gruesome it may be. There may be clues.'

There were several skitterways leading off the Shudders. 'There is Mad Meg Lane,' said Heddsworth, pointing to one. 'The butcher's boy said it was an awful sight. Poor lad. He was terribly ill afterwards, and he still had to make deliveries. I gave him a cup of tea.'

Rose studied the skitterway – its dark winding turns, its cobblestones. As they entered the alley she looked for traces of blood. Someone had sloshed a bucket of water over the site of the attack, but there were still gory rivulets between the stones.

Two police officers stood taking notes. The sergeant, a bearded man with a downturned mouth, looked serious and methodical. A round-faced young constable, who had pink cheeks and prominent ears, stepped forward as the visitors approached. 'You can't come in here,' he warned them. 'This is the scene of a crime.'

'Oh yes, we are aware of that,' said Heddsworth. 'We are very sorry to interrupt your work. But we hoped to be of assistance.'

'Assistance?' said the sergeant. 'Are you witnesses? Did you know the victim? This isn't a place for sightseeing.'

'No, we're not witnesses,' said Rose. 'And we didn't know Moll the Pocket. But we want to help. I am Miss Rose Raventhorpe, and these are my friends.'

The sergeant looked closely at Rose in her white satin dress.

'Well, with respect, Miss Raventhorpe,' said the sergeant, 'this is a police matter. The victim was a criminal, a petty thief. She received some nasty wounds, inflicted by a dog's claws from the look of it. It's not something a young lady should be involved with.'

Bronson scowled, tapping the hilt of her rapier. The constable looked her up and down. 'Excuse me, but are you all carrying weapons?'

Miss Regemont lifted her chin. 'We enjoy the noble sport of fencing, young man. I am Miss Regemont, head of Silvercrest Hall, butlers' academy of Yorke.'

'I see,' said the sergeant coolly. 'Well, I am Sergeant Snodgrass, and this is Constable Murton.' Constable Murton nodded. 'Thank you for your offer of assistance, but we do not need butlers or young ladies to step in. We will find this bloodthirsty beast.'

As he spoke, an unearthly growl came from the depths of Mad Meg Lane.

Rose spun around, hand at her rapier hilt. A huge black hound was pacing towards her, his fangs bared in a snarl.

Chapter 2

The Hound of the Downs

Rose drew her rapier. The butlers flourished their blades. Sergeant Snodgrass drew a pistol.

Charlie Malone held out a warning hand. 'It's all right! I've seen that dog before.'

A woman marched into the skitterway behind the dog. She was tall, with thick red hair and a sharp, intelligent face. Her limbs were sinewy, her skin tanned. Her clothes were distinctly odd – a farmer's coat and a much-patched skirt – but they were good quality, and there was a prim haughtiness about her demeanour that suggested she was more upper class than farm-bred.

'Heel, Wolf!' ordered the woman in crisp, aristocratic tones. The dog obeyed reluctantly.

'I apologise for my dog,' said the woman. 'I don't usually bring him into the city but he gets bad-tempered if I leave him at home. Starts eating pillows.'

'Miss, the dog should be on a leash,' spluttered the sergeant.

'He doesn't like them,' said the woman, glaring at him. 'Do you usually draw a firearm on dogs?'

'Of course not, miss, but there was an attack here last night,' explained Constable Murton. 'A woman was killed. People are frightened. You may attract unwanted attention with your hound.'

'Oh, so that's why people kept staring at us this morning. How ridiculous,' sniffed the woman. 'I rarely come into town, but I had to see that my books had arrived in the shops.'

'Ah!' said Heddsworth. 'You must be Miss Jane

Wildcliffe, the author of *The Bride of Blood Abbey, and Other Gothic Tales* of *Terror.*'

'Oh!' said Rose. 'Miss Wildcliffe! My friend Emily adores your work!'

'Emily Proops?' said Miss Wildcliffe suspiciously. 'The girl who married the young magician? Yes, I've met her and her husband. She still sends me ten admiring letters a week.'

'Yes, that would be Emily,' said Rose, sharing a grin with Orpheus.

'Miss Wildcliffe,' said the Sergeant, with an exasperated look at Rose, 'we must ask – were you or your dog here last night?'

'Of course not!' Miss Wildcliffe looked offended. 'I live out on the moors at Withering Downs. Wolf sleeps at the foot of my bed.'

'Dogs can roam at night,' said the sergeant.

'Mine certainly did not,' Miss Wildcliffe retorted.

The Sergeant cast a mistrustful look at Wolf. 'Can anyone else confirm your dog's whereabouts last night?'

'I live alone,' said Miss Wildcliffe. 'So no, you have only my word for it.'

'Hmm,' said the sergeant, making a note in his book.

'You're the one they call the Moorland Witch, aren't you?' said Constable Murton. 'As a nickname,' he added hastily, in response to the lady's glare.

'I don't go around casting spells,' she retorted. 'If that's what you want to know.'

Sergeant Snodgrass cleared his throat. 'Has the dog ever harmed a person?'

Miss Wildcliffe sighed. 'No, though he would if provoked. In this case the animal is completely innocent.' Her gaze met Rose's. 'I apologise if Wolf scared you.'

'I'm fine,' said Rose. She wasn't entirely convinced of Wolf's innocence – he looked perfectly capable of mauling someone.

Constable Murton frowned. 'You write fiction about demon dogs and suchlike, don't you, Miss

Wildcliffe? Perhaps it would suit you for the old legend to be revived. For publicity.'

'I would hardly go to the lengths of murdering someone to sell books!' Miss Wildcliffe turned an outraged shade of violet. Wolf growled, his hackles raising.

The Sergeant took a step back from the dog. 'She lives alone on the moor,' Rose heard him mutter to his colleague. 'People who live alone too much – well, they can get funny ideas. It's the solitude. I've seen cases like that.' He tapped the side of his head.

'Now look here!' Miss Wildcliffe began. She looked ready to give Sergeant Snodgrass a slap. 'You have no proof I or my dog have done anything wrong.'

Snodgrass cleared his throat with authority. 'No, miss, but we must follow up all lines of inquiry. We will put all our men on to this case. We will search the skitterways, the Muckyards, the dens where people might have rat-killing dogs. The

Lord Mayor will want this creature caught before it hurts anyone else.'

Murton consulted his notebook. 'Have you any family or friends who can testify to the dog's general behaviour, Miss Wildcliffe?'

The authoress scowled and looked away. 'No. Most of my family are dead. Consumption killed my brother and sisters.'

'Grief,' said Constable Murton significantly, 'isn't good for those who brood. Especially ladies living alone.'

Rose tried not to show her annoyance with the constable. 'Was there any other evidence on the victim?'

Murton shook his head. 'No Miss, there were just some stolen things on her. Watches and suchlike. I dare say she planned to take such items to a pawnbroker for money. Someone like Batty Annie in Tatterlace Green—' He quailed at the glare from his superior. 'Ahem. Did you see the sign someone put up outside the skitterway? Seems that people are already talking about old legends like the demon hound. The creature was meant to be summoned by a witch.'

'Fanciful folk tales,' scoffed the sergeant.

'But people do believe in them,' Murton pointed out. 'Yorke is full of old superstitions. You use many of them in your literature – isn't that right, Miss Wildcliffe?'

'I enjoy writing about them, yes,' said Miss Wildcliffe, patting her dog's head.

'Well, our job isn't to do with ghost stories. We're looking for a real dog,' said Snodgrass. He turned to the butlers. 'You don't hold truck with ghost stories, do you?'

'Not at all,' Miss Regemont assured him.

As they talked, Rose took the chance to walk a little further down the alley, scanning bricks and plaster, and moving aside rubbish with her toe. If there were any other clues about, this was the time to find them. She spotted an abandoned lantern, and bent to pick it up.

Then she froze.

A bloody pawprint.

It was the size of her hand, dark red against the cobblestones.

Orpheus sidled up. 'What is it?'

Rose pointed to the pawprint. Orpheus crouched to examine it. The others crowded to look. Charlie Malone whistled.

'It's a big beastie all right,' muttered the Sergeant.

'Big! It's enormous!' sputtered Murton.

'Hmph,' said the Sergeant. Even he looked lost for an explanation. Rose felt a prickle of real fear for the first time since entering Mad Meg Lane. Was it possible that there was a demonic hound? She tried to ignore the thought.

'How did we miss that print?' Constable Murton looked thoroughly unnerved.

'We missed it because we had a dead body to deal with, Murton,' said the Sergeant matter-of-factly. He picked up the abandoned lantern. 'This must have been Moll's, poor girl. Well, it seems we have an uncommonly large dog to catch. I shall have to inform the Lord Mayor.'

'The mayor?' Miss Wildcliffe looked angrier than ever. 'I've no liking for *his* opinions.'

'The mayor needs to know about serious crimes in this city, Miss,' said Snodgrass. Wolf bared his fangs, and Murton stepped quickly away.

'For heaven's sake man, don't be a coward,' said the woman impatiently. 'Here, the children can come and pet him. He loves having his ears pulled.'

Rose wasn't thrilled by the invitation, and from the look on his face Orpheus wasn't either. She moved her hand very slowly towards the dog's head, ready to snatch it back. 'Good boy,' she muttered, and gave Wolf's ears a quick pat. Orpheus did the same, leaning in gingerly from a distance. Rose dared to look at Wolf's paws. They were certainly big, but were they as large as the print on the cobblestones? She doubted it – Wolf's paws would only be half that size.

'I think it's time we cleared the scene,' Snodgrass announced. 'We can't finish our work with a crowd around. You may go, Miss Wildcliffe. But I would like you to stay close to Yorke so we can contact you for any further questioning. And keep that dog at home – for its own good if nothing else. People are spooked after what's happened here.'

Miss Wildcliffe tightened her hold on her dog's furry neck. 'I don't understand how anyone could think Wolf is dangerous.'

Wolf spotted a pigeon strutting on a windowsill. Slaver dripped from his jaws.

'No,' said Orpheus, under his breath. 'I can't imagine why.'

Miss Wildcliffe left the skitterway with her pet, followed by Rose and her friends. Rose noticed that the authoress attracted hostile glances from the people she passed. She was not sure how many of them were due to Wolf and how many to the woman's witchy, eccentric appearance.

'Well, the police are trying at least,' Miss

Regemont said with a sigh. 'I suppose many officers wouldn't care about the death of a mere pickpocket.'

'Shall we make inquiries in the Shudders?' Heddsworth pointed down the street. 'Perhaps someone there saw the dog. Miss Regemont, you could talk to the staff at Glyph and Brackett's Bookshop. Bronson could visit Dorabella's tea rooms. I can inquire at the Pythagorean Cup Tavern, and Mr Malone at the draper's. Miss Raventhorpe and Master Orpheus, perhaps—' Heddsworth paused. 'Is that a new establishment?'

They all stared down the street. A new shop-front had appeared near the bookshop. Its sign announced THE YORKE CHOCOLATE EMPORIUM. In smaller writing were the words: SENSATIONAL SWEETS FOR SPECIAL OCCASIONS.

'We'll go there,' Rose and Orpheus chorused, and grinned at each other. They might be looking for a savage dog, but there was no reason why they couldn't investigate a chocolate shop as well.

Chapter 3

The Yorke Chocolate Emporium

The shop was decorated in crimson and gold stripes, and its window display was mouth-watering. A chocolate grandfather clock stood in one corner, near a chocolate replica of Yorke Minster. There were chocolate cups holding foamy chocolate mousse. Sweets of all colours and sizes glowed like rainbows in crystal jars. Scents of lemon, vanilla and violet sugar wafted across the street. A whole pack of people gazed longingly into the window.

The door opened, and a portly, red-cheeked man smiled shyly at the crowd. 'We will open in a few minutes. Then you may try our free samples.'

He met Rose's eye and smiled in recognition. She squealed. 'Lorimer!'

Rose had met Lorimer the butler last autumn, while investigating a murder. He was the kindly, timid and overworked assistant to Dr Jankers, the 'Doctor of Dissection' and owner of the Yorke Medical School.

'What are you doing here?' Rose wanted to know. 'Have you left the Medical School? Dr Jankers didn't fire you, did he?'

'Oh no, miss. We have started a new business! I have convinced Dr Jankers to start a sideline in confectionery,' said Lorimer. 'Would you and your friend do us the honour of coming in? I would love your opinion on the new shop.'

Rose and Orpheus drew envious looks as they

slipped through the door. Lorimer locked it behind him, and waved a hand at the shop's interior. 'What do you think?'

'Heavenly,' said Rose.

Bowls, jars and beribboned boxes of chocolates filled every nook. The smell of chocolate, caramel, raspberry cream and barley sugar was intoxicating.

'This is my friend Orpheus,' Rose told Lorimer. 'Orpheus, this is Lorimer.'

'Oh yes, the young man who lives at the Hall!' cried Lorimer. 'A pleasure to meet you. You must take some chocolates home for your sister and yourself.'

'Thank you!' said Orpheus fervently.

Dr Jankers himself appeared at the shop door.

'Oh, hello.' The doctor peered at them fiercely through his spectacles, and stroked his ginger sideburns. 'Bit of a change, this business! I must say I thought Lorimer was barking mad at first, suggesting this venture. We started with marshmallow-flavoured medicine, and it led to this.'

'I'm sure it will be very profitable,' said Rose, as the customers outside the windows ogled the displays.

The doctor harrumphed. 'One hopes so, Miss Raventhorpe. I will continue my work at the Medical School, and allow Lorimer his little enterprise. I am here only as a financial and business advisor. Toffee's dratted hard to get right.'

'Mmmmm,' said Orpheus, halfway through a box of free samples. 'I'll be your taste tester.'

'We're actually here about an attack that took place last night,' explained Rose. 'Have you heard about it yet?'

'Oh yes,' said Lorimer with a shiver. 'The Barghest of legend, the bier-ghost, the death-hound of Yorke. A witch has summoned it from the grave to stalk the streets and claim a new victim.'

'The Barghest?' said Rose, startled. 'The dog

that killed Mad Meg a hundred years ago? Surely you don't believe in that? Not to mention witches!'

'The Barghest!' said the doctor, with a sniff. 'That's all mere legend, Lorimer. Last night's unfortunate attack was the result of an ill-trained hunting dog on the loose, nothing more.'

'What dog?' asked another voice. A young woman entered the room from a back door, carrying a tray of violet creams. 'Good morning,' she said, seeing the children. 'We're not open yet.'

'Thank you, Sylvia,' said Dr Jankers. 'These two are Miss Raventhorpe and Master – what is it? – Orpheus. They're paying an early visit.'

'How do you do?' said Sylvia, disposing of the tray. 'I'm Sylvia Prentiss. The new assistant.'

Rose and Orpheus said hello. Sylvia was a tall, thin, severe-looking girl in a neat white apron.

'I am Dr Jankers' niece,' she told them. 'He kindly allowed me to work here.'

'You're lucky,' said Orpheus. 'I'd eat too much chocolate.'

'I do not care to eat chocolate,' said Sylvia primly. 'It is more instructive to work with it. We shall open in two and a half minutes, Mr Lorimer.'

'Thank you.' Lorimer smiled at the children. 'Very handy girl. Very helpful.'

Very glum, Rose thought. But then, she seemed the sort of person who would be observant too. 'Did you hear about the attack last night, Sylvia?' she asked. She watched the girl's face for any change of expression, but Sylvia barely blinked. Rose might have been talking about the weather.

'Oh, you mean the dog attack? Quite unpleasant,' said Sylvia. 'But look at the crowds out there! Any publicity is good for our business. We will sell a great amount of chocolate today.'

'Quite,' said Rose, trying to hide her disgust. 'Did you see or hear anything that might explain what happened? The dog must have come from somewhere.'

'I don't pay much attention to stray dogs,' said Sylvia, with a shrug. 'And that woman shouldn't have been out in the skitterway at that time of night, stealing from honest folk. Only those up to no good are out that late. Theft gives the area a bad name. It will keep customers away.'

'It's not her fault she was murdered,' said Rose coldly. 'I don't like thieving either, but for some people it's that or starvation.'

'Or the workhouse,' said Orpheus quietly. 'Or orphanages.'

'Mmm. Very sad,' said Sylvia in a disinterested tone. 'I'm simply being honest. Business will be excellent today all around the Shudders, with flocks of people coming to look at the site of the death. You're here because of it, aren't you?' Before Rose could make an indignant reply, Sylvia took her place at the till. 'We are ready to open the shop now, Mr Lorimer. Do you wish to return to the Medical School, Uncle? Mr Lorimer and I will manage, I'm sure.'

Rose and Orpheus left the shop, carrying their complimentary basket of chocolates. They struggled through the press of eager customers entering the Emporium.

'Phew,' said Orpheus, straightening his hat. 'That Sylvia. She ought to sell fish, not chocolate!'

'Let's hope the others had more luck,' Rose said.

They walked down the Shudders and found their friends. The butlers were not in the best of moods.

'People can't stop talking gossip instead of sense,' groaned Bronson. 'How it must be the Barghest returned to haunt Mad Meg Lane, how it had red, blazing eyes, and was seen floating through a brick wall.' She rolled her eyes. 'No real information about real dogs.'

'Superstitions run thick about that lane,' agreed Charlie Malone. 'Everyone's telling a story about a time they saw a ghost or a spirit or a hobgoblin.'

'Nobody seems to have seen anything genuinely relating to the murder,' sighed Miss Regemont. 'We shall have to question people about the city, to learn who has a vicious type of dog.'

Bronson glanced at the bookshop display. 'Well, that will not help the situation,' she said in exasperation.

They all looked at the window. Miss Wildcliffe's latest book was prominently displayed. The cover showed a ferocious, red-eyed hound.

They heard a piercing squeal behind them. Rose's friend Emily and her husband Harry Dodge were standing in the street.

'Oh, her latest is out at last!' Emily exclaimed. 'How utterly thrilling. Now we shall learn more about the Barghest of Yorke.'

'Emily!' Rose rushed to her. 'Could you not talk too loudly about victims? There has been a vicious dog attack.'

'Yes, we heard. Frightful news!' agreed Harry. 'We hoped to see you here. I feared it would be risky for Emily in her condition, but she insisted on coming to get the new book. We're both great admirers of Miss Wildcliffe. Visited her house once in our hot-air balloon.'

Sixteen-year-old Emily's pregnancy was discreetly concealed. She wore a velvet cape over her pink-and-black striped dress, and a hat with a black feather. She showed Rose a brooch made from the hair of friends and relatives. 'I shall add the baby's as soon as it has enough hair,' she told her friend. 'I hope it has night-dark hair and sea-green eyes, just like the heroine of *The Nightmare Corpse's Curse.* We have been reading Gothic poetry aloud to educate the baby.'

'And I've decorated the nursery,' said Harry proudly. 'Purple satin cradle, a trapeze from the theatre, and pictures of top hats and rabbits.'

'Very striking,' said Orpheus, trying to keep a straight face.

'Yes,' said Emily, beaming. 'Now what is all this talk about the poor girl being taken by the dog? It's dreadful. I wonder if she saw the Barghest before it took her life? It must have been terrifying.'

'The Barghest?' said Rose. 'Honestly, Emily!'

But Emily was off again. 'People are not always savaged when they encounter the Barghest, you see. Merely sighting the red-eyed dog can make some people die on the spot with fright.'

'How very kind of the Barghest to give people that option,' said Bronson sarcastically. 'I fear that Moll the Pocket was not so lucky.'

'It has all sorts of names,' Emily continued, ignoring Bronson. 'Some call it Skriker, or the Black Shuck, or—'

'We could do something with it onstage,' said Harry. 'At the Clarion!' He leaned forward, eyes alight. '*The Death-Hound of the Shudders* would bring them in by the hundreds!'

'No,' snapped Bronson. 'Don't you dare. It's shocking bad taste!'

'Maybe you're right,' sighed Harry. 'But we could tone down some aspects. I'm sure we could manage it. Would you consider joining the theatre, Orpheus? You're a dashing-looking lad.'

'Oh yes,' said Emily happily. 'You could play

a Saracen in our production of *The Knights of the Round Table*.'

'Um,' said Orpheus. 'Thank you. Very kind.'

'We could make a ghostly dog to go in the production,' Harry enthused. 'It would be easy to do the red eyes. A scrap of red fabric or paper covering a lamp, like a Hallow's Eve jack o' lantern – just the ticket.'

'You're so clever, darling,' praised Emily. 'Now, we'd better go to the bookshop before all the books are sold out.' She waved a cheerful goodbye to Rose and her friends, and they dived through the bookshop doors. Rose hoped Miss Wildcliffe had left the vicinity.

Miss Regemont checked her pocket watch. 'It seems we have nothing new to learn here. We shall have to make further enquiries and keep an eye out for dogs while we are patrolling the city. Come along, Bronson, Mr Malone. Orpheus, are you returning with us?'

'I'd like to look into this mystery a little more,' said Rose. 'Can you stay, Orpheus?'

'If you like,' he agreed. 'What about you, Heddsworth?'

'I need to return to Lambsgate and see to lunch preparations,' said Heddsworth. He frowned. 'What exactly are you going to do, Miss Raventhorpe?'

'Ask a few questions, that sort of thing,' said Rose.

'Oh, indeed?' said Heddsworth. 'See that you do not get into trouble, and return in time for lunch.'

'I will,' Rose promised.

When Heddsworth and the others had gone, Rose stood twirling her cameo necklace around her fingers.

'What is it?' asked Orpheus. 'Your brain's like a pocket watch. Tick, tick, tick. Lucky for you I'm such a patient and brilliant person.'

'Ha ha,' said Rose. 'I was thinking. There was a lantern left behind at the scene of the attack. Sergeant Snodgrass thought it was Moll's, but what if it wasn't? Maybe someone was there that night with the savage dog. A person could deliberately have set a dog on Moll the Pocket. You know, instead of a dog running wild and attacking someone at random. Dogs can be trained to attack. Maybe someone went after her to get their stolen goods back. Maybe someone meant the dog to kill her, or at least hurt her.'

'Set a dog on her deliberately?' Orpheus sounded disbelieving. 'You mean murder?'

'It's possible,' Rose argued. 'And if that is what happened, we need to think about who might have wanted Moll dead. One of the people she pickpocketed on a previous night, maybe.'

'I think you're a bit too keen on solving murders,' said Orpheus. 'A dog attacked her. A real one, not a ghost. That's all.'

'Well, I think it's worth following up,' said Rose stubbornly. 'That constable mentioned a woman called Batty Annie. Do you know anything about her?'

'Oh, her! Batty Annie runs a second-hand goods shop off Tatterlace Green,' said Orpheus. 'She's the Junkyard Queen. People pawn stuff with her.'

'Well, perhaps – if there was a murderer – he or she was after something that Moll had stolen and pawned to Batty Annie,' said Rose. 'It's worth talking to her at least.'

Orpheus shrugged, and grinned. 'All right. A fool's errand more like, but I fancy a walk through the Stairs Below.'

'Yes,' said Rose happily. 'Where is the nearest door? Let's take the one off Cornsgate.'

They walked to the pretty street of Cornsgate and found the small, unimportant-looking door. It was one of many scattered throughout the city, leading to the underground tunnels used by the Silvercrest Hall butlers. It was not always an easy way to travel. You needed a good sense of direction and knowledge of all the branching pathways – but Rose loved being part of this hidden world. It was a means for the Guardians of Yorke to protect their city.

As soon as they were sure they were unwatched, Rose used her Infinity Key to open the door. Orpheus lit one of the lanterns kept behind the door with matches from his pocket. Rose locked the door, and they set off down the steps into the narrow passage.

Navigating the Stairs Below was a tricky business. You could open a door to see where you were, but doors did not always appear when you needed them. Rose and Orpheus both carried compasses, and consulted them when necessary.

'Right,' said Orpheus, after one such session of compass study, 'we should be near the Clarion Theatre. If we take the next door out we'll find Tatterlace Green.'

They opened the next door cautiously, checking no one was looking, and slipped through it, locking it behind them. It was eleven o'clock, and few people visited the theatres lining the street at this time of day. The shops beyond them were shabby, for this was not a fashionable part of Yorke.

The people about looked shabby too – pinch-faced, tired and careworn. It was a place where seamstresses, laundresses and coal-sellers made a hard living. Orpheus swivelled on his heel for a moment, getting his bearings, before pointing. 'There it is! Bits, Bobs and Bric-a-Brac. Come on. Let's see what we can learn from Batty Annie.'

Chapter 4

The Unwatched Watch

The tiny shop looked like it would burst at the seams. China, hat-brushes, chamber pots, bellows, wax flowers, beads, snuff-boxes and powder puffs crammed the shelves. One shelf was full of lone, unpaired shoes – even beribboned ladies' boots and fisherman's waders. Rose squeezed her way around hairless dolls and books with missing pages. Cracked mirrors and broken parasols dangled from the ceiling on strings. Rose smelled leather, old paper, stale perfume and dust.

She felt as if she had stumbled into a magpie's nest.

A woman with a pinched face, a creased felt hat and skirts that appeared more mud than fabric sat in a corner, looking as if she had lived there for ever. Reposing on a pile of patched cushions, she smelled of mould and earth and pipe-smoke. 'Morning, dears,' she said, and smiled toothlessly at Orpheus. He swept off his hat and bowed to her.

'Ah, the sailor's boy!' she exclaimed. 'Orpheus the Orphan. I remember when your pa came in here. When 'e was still alive, that is. Good man, tryin' to help your sick sister.'

Orpheus nodded. 'Yes,' he said quietly. 'I remember. Annie, this is Miss Rose Raventhorpe. We – we have just come from the Shudders, where all the talk is of this terrible attack. We wondered if you knew Moll the Pocket.'

Annie nodded. 'Yes, I knew her, you might say. She were my niece,' she said gruffly. 'A right rapscallion, but she didn't deserve no savagin'.'

Orpheus winced. 'My deepest sympathies, ma'am.'

'Oh!' said Rose. 'I'm so sorry.'

Batty Annie looked away. 'She took too many risks, that girl. I told her that. Especially in that lane.' She looked back at them. 'It's the Barghest that took her,' she said matter-of-factly.

Rose stared at the woman. 'Don't you think it's more likely to have been a real dog?'

'Oh, but the Barghest is real, Miss Raventhorpe.' Batty Annie's voice took on a strange, deep quality. 'You've seen what the cats o' Yorke can do, haven't you?'

Rose gasped. She had never heard anyone apart from the butlers speak of the cats' magical powers.

'So why don't you believe in the Barghest?' asked Batty Annie.

'The cats are different!' spluttered Rose, still shocked by Annie's knowledge. 'I haven't seen any evidence of a supernatural dog.'

Batty Annie rummaged under the counter and brought out an ancient chest. With a flick of locks she opened it and took out some very peculiar objects. A huge, studded dog collar. A Celtic torc with wolf-heads at the tips. A tattered Viking banner depicting a wolf-like skull. A newspaper cutting from the last century, warning of a beast spotted in local graveyards. And a recent article from the *Yorke Tribune* describing a train crash, accompanied by a sketch of an evil-eyed hound. Rose remembered hearing about the crash several months ago – people had been killed, and the Lord Mayor had been injured. It had made all the papers. Even Lady Raventhorpe had been affected by the news, enough to organise a charity ball for the local hospital.

The Barghest foretells death and doom!' the article read. 'People heard the beast howl hours before last week's railway crash. Two signalmen disabled. A brave policeman left in mourning as his infant daughter Katie perished with her mother.

Three young men maimed for life, and the Lord Mayor himself suffering a broken leg. Could it have been prevented? DID THE HOUND OF THE SKITTERWAYS KNOW?'

'Well, that's just gruesome,' Rose muttered. She looked at the photographs, the faces of those poor people now dead. A pretty young woman held a baby in a white frilly dress. Perhaps it had been the baby's first train ride. And here was this article focusing on a ghostly beast. 'How can anyone believe that?' she demanded. 'A dog howls in the street, and people decide that it foretold an accident?'

'What is all this stuff?' asked Orpheus, peering at the dog collar.

'The history of the Barghest,' said Batty Annie. 'You see how many tales are told of him? All the different forms he takes over the centuries? He is no easy creature to defeat, bein' immortal.'

'But—' began Rose.

Annie gazed at her. 'You've felt his presence,

haven't you? And you'll meet him, my dear. Soon enough.'

Rose felt the hairs rise on the back of her neck. Orpheus stepped protectively in front of her. 'Don't say that,' he ordered Batty Annie. 'Rose wants to help you, to find the dog that killed Moll. It's just coincidence that it happened in Mad Meg Lane.'

Batty Annie hissed through her teeth. 'That lane! I wish Moll'd stuck to the Muckyards. But there's rich pickin's in the Shudders late at night.'

'We understand,' said Rose. 'Did she leave many things with you? Can we see them?'

Batty Annie glanced at her challengingly. 'Are you goin' to the police about 'em?'

'No, no.' Rose held out her hands. 'Moll is dead, and the police can't do anything to her – or you, I hope.'

Batty Annie still seemed mistrustful. But she reached under the counter again and fished out a battered box. She drew out a handful of items – a gold fob watch, four silk handkerchiefs, two pipes, and a pair of spectacles in a satin-lined case.

Rose inspected them. The handkerchiefs were not monogrammed, giving her no clue as to who might have owned them. The spectacle case was unmarked. But the fob watch was inscribed on the back: *R. Rawlings.*

'Who is this Rawlings?' Rose mused aloud.

The Junkyard Queen sucked in her cheeks. 'Moll spoke of 'im. Picked 'is pocket only a week ago, around midnight. A hefty feller. He wasn't drunk, but she still managed to nick his watch. One of them butlers by 'is dress.'

'A butler?' gasped Rose.

'Aye,' said Batty Annie. 'Midnight, it was, but there was enough moonlight that night for her to see 'im.'

Rose and Orpheus exchanged swift glances. 'Is there a Rawlings at the Hall?' Rose asked him quietly.

He shook his head. 'No. But it's likely they'll know of him if he's a butler.'

'Can you tell us anything else about Moll?' Rose asked Annie.

Batty Annie took the watch from Rose and pushed the box out of sight. 'Nothin' more of her to tell. But if it's the Barghest you want to destroy, you need the sword of Sigandus. The sword that belongs to the true defenders of Yorke. Only a true guardian of the city can take that from the rock where it is hidden. It's got a blade sharp enough to cut a hole in walls.'

'A sword that can cut through walls?' Rose was bewildered. 'Where is it supposed to be?'

Batty Annie laughed, and folded her hands under her chin. Then she chanted:

The king he came to Yorke one day
A silver blade he gave away
Where now it lies nobody tells
It sleeps within the sound of bells.

Great its power, strong its call
Sharp enough to cleave a wall.
True defender, you alone
shall break Sigandus from the stone.
Many would its master be
But only one may pull it free.

'A sword hidden within the sound of bells?' said Rose. 'Does that mean the cathedral bells, I wonder? They can be heard all over Yorkesborough.'

'The sword 'as powers,' said Batty Annie, in a compelling voice. 'Though it's lost, perhaps you will find it and use it to dispatch the beast. Be warned, it is not wise to seek it too long. There are those who become obsessed by it.'

Rose stifled a groan. She needed to find the dog, and possibly the grudging owner, that had killed Moll the Pocket – not a legendary sword!

'Thank you, Annie. We should go now,' said Orpheus courteously. Rose said a polite goodbye and they left the shop.

'I'd like to find this Rawlings,' Rose decided, as they stood outside on the pavement. 'He wasn't pickpocketed on the night of Moll's death, but he could still be a suspect. He could have been there last night too, and attacked Moll then.'

'You think he took revenge on Moll for stealing his watch?' Orpheus gave a sceptical snort. 'It was just a watch, not his life savings.'

'All right, that's true. But it could have been very precious to him,' Rose suggested. 'Perhaps he realised it was Moll who had robbed him. He could have bought a guard dog, and gone back to Mad Meg Lane at night to seek revenge on her.'

Orpheus shook his head. 'I doubt it.'

'Well, I'd still like to talk to him. And what on earth was that sword story about? And all that superstition about the Barghest! Doesn't Annie understand that a real dog killed her niece?'

'She's a strange old thing,' said Orpheus. He kicked an apple core off the pavement. 'But that poem is interesting. The "sound of bells" would suit the Hall, wouldn't it? They have bells there, for the student butlers learning to wait on people.'

Rose was startled to realise that he had a point. The Hall was full of bells. 'But then,' Orpheus mused, 'if the sword was at the Hall, someone would have found it by now. Inaaya would have, she thinks the place belongs to her. The butlers spoil her rotten. Did you know she's their official scone taster now?'

At the word 'scone', Rose's stomach growled. They both giggled.

'You'd better go home for lunch,' said Orpheus. 'Can you come to Silvercrest Hall with Heddsworth tomorrow? Swords are the butlers' specialty. If anyone will know about Sigandus, it's them.'

'Reynard Rawlings?' said Heddsworth over lunch at Lambsgate half an hour later. 'But of course I know who he is. The Lord Mayor's butler!'

Rose was agog. 'The Lord Mayor! And he's not from Silvercrest Hall?'

Heddsworth nodded. 'Not every butler in Yorke is, Miss Raventhorpe. But it is very strange that Moll the Pocket should have stolen his watch. Why would a respectable butler like him be out in a skitterway late at night?'

'Perhaps he had some good reason for being out,' suggested Rose.

'Perhaps,' said Heddsworth thoughtfully. 'He seems devoted to the mayor. Treats him as if he was a genuine duke, not just a railway king.'

Rose knew of the mayor, Sir Edward Chesney, from her father. Sir Edward, the 'Duke of the Railways', had built up a fortune developing railroads in Yorkesborough. Suddenly, travel to London and other cities had become astonishingly fast. People had rushed to invest in the enterprise. But it was a risky undertaking. Sir Edward liked to spend money, eager to build more railways. He had been injured in the recent train accident that made the papers. Rose remembered the article she had read at Batty Annie's, mentioning the rumours of the Barghest howling to warn of the crash. But the mayor had survived that accident, although he was confined to a bath chair until his broken leg healed. Yet he still insisted that the train was the way of the future. There was no stopping Mayor Chesney. The fact that his butler had been in a skitterway late at night was very interesting indeed.

The next day, when Heddsworth had completed his duties at Rose's home, he travelled with her to the Hall to meet Orpheus. He led her into a spacious classroom, where they found Miss Regemont hard at work with her trainee butlers. Steam looked as if it was coming out of her ears, but it was only from her iron. She was holding a lesson on the correct way to iron newspapers – one of a skilled butler's duties. Bronson and Charlie Malone had joined in to help the younger students.

Rose and Orpheus were given their own irons and told to try their skill.

'So Rawlings was in a skitterway in the middle of the night?' Miss Regemont said, once Rose had shared their news. 'I don't understand. Why would he do such a thing?'

'I don't know,' said Rose, struggling with her iron. 'But I think it's odd. He is definitely a suspect. Oh – and Batty Annie said something about a sword. She repeated a rhyme about the sword of Sigandus – the only weapon that can defeat the Barghest. It was lost, somewhere among the sound of bells. Another legend. Do you know anything about it?'

Miss Regemont raised her eyebrows. 'That sword! It was lost five hundred years ago. A king gave it to our founding butler, Arlington, as thanks for allowing him to stay at Silvercrest Hall while London was suffering from the plague. It vanished soon afterwards. Stolen, most likely. Of course there is an old legend saying that a true defender of Yorke would be able to find it. But who knows where it is now?'

Charlie Malone finished ironing his newspaper and folded it into the shape of a swan. 'It was probably lost down a well somewhere, or sold for scrap,' he said.

'Five hundred years!' said Rose. 'Are there any records about it? Any stories or rumours?'

'None that I know of. Disappeared in history,' said Charlie.

'I believe I've seen a book about it in the library,' said Heddsworth. 'I shall search for it.'

All the butlers were trying to iron their copies of the paper without setting them on fire, creasing them, or becoming distracted by the headlines. Rose found a picture of her mother in the society pages. She felt awkward about ironing over her face. Orpheus ironed his pages neatly and folded them into the shape of a ship for his sister Inaaya, who played at sailing it around the room.

'Have you discovered any vicious dogs, madam?' Heddsworth asked Miss Regemont.

'Not yet. We shall continue to investigate – such a creature cannot be easy to hide.'

Charlie Malone paused as he lifted his iron. 'Wait a minute,' he said. 'Read this.'

They crowded to look at the page. The headline was: **WAKEMEN TO KEEP WATCH ON WALL**.

In the aftermath of a recent violent attack in the Shudders, the Lord Mayor, Sir Edward Chesney, is to boost our city's security by appointing a number of the professional thief-takers of London, also known as the Wakemen, to patrol the walls and streets.

'The Wakemen are respectable gentlemen who are practised in arms,' said the Mayor. 'Our police force is struggling to investigate this case. With the aid of the Wakemen I hope to quell rebellious ruffians, robbery and rumours, and find the dog responsible for the attack in the Shudders. Violent crime must be stopped in this city, and the Wakemen have promised to find the creature and put an end to its vicious behaviour.

'The Wakemen!' Charlie Malone set down his iron. 'I've heard about that lot – they're nothing but bullies. They insist on people paying money for "protection", but it's only to line their own pockets. If they caught the dog that killed Moll it would be all right – but they'll only stir up more trouble.'

'Wonderful,' sighed Bronson. 'Just what we need. What is Mayor Chesney thinking?'

Rose set down her iron. 'Orpheus and I will go out to the city walls,' she decided. 'We will look for the Wakemen and report back on what they are up to. I want to learn if they really mean to catch the dog, and how they intend to go about it.'

'Well said, Miss Raventhorpe,' Heddsworth declared. 'But should we not go with you?'

'No, it's quite all right. It's broad daylight, Heddsworth! I'm sure it will be safe.'

Rose saw Orpheus glance sidewise at her. He knew she no longer felt completely comfortable up on the city walls. *Well, I will not stop going up there,* Rose told herself. *I won't fall prey to superstition. My role is as a Guardian of Yorke, and if anyone belongs up there I do.*

Chapter 5

Crossed Blades

Once she was up on the walls, Rose decided to ignore all forebodings. She hummed under her breath. She admired the view. She fought the edginess creeping up her spine.

'Feeling better?' said Orpheus, sauntering along a stretch of wall.

'I was just under the weather before,' lied Rose.

'Don't let Heddsworth hear you say that. He'll make you take his tonic-infused tea.'

'Oh, please no,' said Rose. That tea tasted like rotten herrings and seaweed.

Suddenly Orpheus tensed. 'Look.'

Two men strode towards them on the wall. They wore grey fur cloaks and black jet badges on their shoulders, the stones fashioned in the shape of paws. More alarmingly, they carried swords and made no effort to hide them.

'Hey,' one called belligerently to the children. 'What are you doing up here? Nobody allowed on the wall without authorisation. Lord Mayor's orders.'

Rose stared at the man. His puffy face enclosed pebble-cold eyes. 'The Lord Mayor's orders?' she repeated.

'We're the Wakemen,' said the man. 'Elected by the mayor. I am Glyde, and this is Bathory, otherwise known as the Black Dog. We've been hired to find a vicious hound.' He narrowed his eyes at the children's weapons. 'And we can arrest or fine anyone suspected of wrongdoing. Carrying weapons, for instance.'

'We're not hurting anyone,' said Rose. 'And we want to find the vicious dog too.'

The other Wakeman, Bathory, who was handsome in a cold, sneering way, took a money pouch from his belt. 'I don't like people carrying weapons without our permission. Being as you're a young lady I'll let you go with a warning, but I'll have to fine your servant boy there two shillings. It's worth it to have our protection from the savage dog.'

'Orpheus is not my servant!' Rose was so angry she thought the stone would crack under her feet. 'And we have every right to be here. *You* have no right to demand money from us. We will not pay your so-called *fine*.'

'And she's Lord Raventhorpe's daughter, if that means anything to you,' said Orpheus.

'Ooh,' said Bathory, raising his eyebrows. 'A lord's daughter, eh? Well, we'll make it six shillings then.' He held out his hand. 'Pay up.'

'No,' said Rose. She pointed to the city. 'Go

and hunt down real criminals, if you want to be useful at all.'

Bathory smirked. 'Either you pay or we'll confiscate your weapons. I wouldn't recommend fighting us. We'd cut you to ribbons. Terrible tragedy.' His gaze narrowed, and he looked eagerly at the rapiers. 'What kind of swords are they?'

Glyde studied their weapons, then shook his head at his colleague. 'Look at the hilts on 'em. They're just rapiers. Not old like the one in the rhyme.'

'What did you say?' said Rose alertly. 'What kind of sword are you looking for?'

'One better than those toy blades,' said Bathory. He gazed out over the city, eyes alight with longing. 'It's powerful. It makes you a defender of this whole city.'

Glyde grunted. 'It would if you could find it, but it doesn't exist. It's just a nursery rhyme, a fairy tale.'

'Fairy tale?' Orpheus gaped at them. 'You're looking for the sword of Sigandus?'

Bathory stepped forward. 'So you know of it, boy? Yes, I'd like to get my hands on that. If you know where it is, I'll let you carry weapons any time you like.'

'Of course we don't have the sword of Sigandus,' Rose retorted. 'And we are not giving you our rapiers either!'

Bathory scowled. He stepped forward, hand on the hilt of his own blade.

'Do you mean to fight us? You against a couple of children?' challenged Orpheus. 'Even the mayor won't like that.'

Glyde pointed his sword at Orpheus's throat. 'I don't put up with rudeness from brats, even if they do have fancy friends.'

Rose glanced quickly around. There were no other people on the wall, and nobody visible on the street below. There were no witnesses if the Wakemen wanted to hurt them. Her hands were cold with fear, and she badly wanted to turn and run. Only pride and anger kept her from that. If Orpheus got hurt, she would make those Wakemen suffer!

As she was just beginning to fear that they would have to pay the Wakemen, a cat slunk up on to the wall. It was Rose's cat, Watchful. Pitch-black, with golden eyes, he rubbed Orpheus's leg with his nose. Then he hissed at the Wakemen.

Bathory waved his sword at the cat. 'Back to the alley, fleabag.'

Watchful extended his claws, leapt past the sword, and scratched Bathory's arm.

As Bathory swung the sword, Watchful leapt right off the wall. He twisted his body, arched his back, and landed as easily as if the cobblestones were feather pillows. Taking advantage of the distraction, Rose and Orpheus bolted away from the Wakemen, back down the steps.

'Run away then!' shouted Bathory. 'Go on, your Ladyship! If I catch you up here again you'll have more than a fine to pay!'

*

They took the Stairs Below to Silvercrest Hall, where Miss Regemont served them tea in her office and the butlers raged against the Wakemen.

'Just how many of these louts has the mayor hired?' Miss Regemont demanded. 'It's a disgrace! To threaten children!' Her kettle sizzled as she poured boiling water into a teapot. 'Thief-takers my eye,' she muttered. 'Greedy bullies, more like! Mayor Chesney is a fool to think them suitable for peacekeeping.'

'They'd better not try fining any of us,' growled Charlie Malone. 'Or we'll show them what real Guardians are capable of.'

Rose toyed with her teacup. 'Bathory wants the sword because he thinks it's powerful. We should find it before he does. He would never hand it over to the mayor or you butlers.'

'I know where Chesney is today,' said Bronson. She took a perfectly ironed newspaper from Miss Regemont's desk. 'There is an article about him here. He is to attend the cathedral at eleven for a special service.'

'Will his butler be with him?' wondered Rose. 'I'd love to ask Rawlings a few questions about his missing watch.'

'We shall see,' said Heddsworth, reaching for the walking stick that enclosed his rapier. 'This time I'm going with you. I don't want you meeting those Wakemen again alone.'

'Have you butlers had any luck searching for the dog?' Orpheus asked.

'No,' said Bronson, frowning. 'But people are very edgy out there, especially around the Shudders. They seem to be convinced that there is a demon hound out there. Somehow the rumour of that big pawprint has got out. They're all talking about the Barghest. The sooner we find the real dog the better.'

Within the sound of bells.

Rose sat with her friends in a pew of the

magnificent cathedral, her brain whirring. What if the riddle had nothing to do with the Hall and everything to do with these great bells? After all, where in all Yorkesborough were there bells so famous? Every Sunday they rang out, clear through the fog, pealing across to the moors. It seemed a fitting place for a historic sword to be hidden. So where might it be?

The crypt, she thought. Or the Archbishop's office. But it couldn't be anywhere too obvious. Some of the statues of saints carried swords, but they were marble, not steel. Near the bells themselves, then?

She gazed upwards, and saw the grinning gargoyles of the cathedral's interior. There were snarling jaws and paws stretched out to attack. Of course, gargoyles were meant to be dark and devilish in their appearance, but Rose felt a fresh, unsettling sense of menace.

Sigandus belongs to the true defenders of Yorke, she thought. She touched the cat-carved cameo on her necklace. *I won't have the Wakemen finding it first.*

'There's the mayor with Rawlings,' whispered Heddsworth. 'In the next pew.'

Rose tilted her head to take a better look. The mayor looked square-jawed and severe, well dressed in a tweed jacket and silk waistcoat. Rawlings matched Batty Annie's description. He was a massively built man, whose muscles strained under his butler's tailcoat. He looked more like a boxer than a butler. But as Rose stared at him, he took out a tiny, pristine handkerchief in his gloved hands, and daintily dusted the top of the pew.

The Archbishop began his sermon. 'Our beloved city has a great history,' he said, 'rich with legends and fascinating detail. But, dear people of Yorkesborough, beware of falling prey to superstition. We often hear tales of violence and tragedy. It is tempting to open our hearts to fear. But this is no excuse to panic, or believe ancient tales rather than the plain truth of things. I have heard rumours of witches and supernatural hounds. Remember, there are no demonic monsters in this city, nothing worse than our own faults and failings.'

Rose was glad to hear this, considering people's talk of the Barghest. Covertly, she looked around the congregation, trying to read their mood. Many looked troubled, uneasy, anxious. Her heart sank.

She spent the rest of the service watching Rawlings. He sang the hymns and listened serenely to the sermon. She noticed that he wore no fob watch. Had he indeed been robbed by Moll the Pocket? Why else would Batty Annie possess a stolen watch engraved with his name?

When the sermon ended and the congregation began to file out, Heddsworth led the children to the mayor's pew. The mayor was talking to the Archbishop, so Heddsworth addressed his butler. 'How do you do, Rawlings? This is his Lordship's daughter, Miss Rose Raventhorpe, and her friend Orpheus Rayburn, or Raven. They wish for an audience with the mayor if he can spare a moment.'

'Ah, Miss Raventhorpe. Master Raven.' Rawlings bowed politely. 'A pleasure.' Close up, he had a square face and hawklike eyes, the face of a soldier. Perhaps he had been a soldier before he became a butler. A strong man. A man who would set a dog on a pickpocket?

'We only want to talk to the mayor for a minute or two,' said Rose. 'We must not be late for lunch. Do you know the time, Rawlings?' she said innocently. 'I haven't a watch.'

The man moved as if to check, and then stopped. 'I do apologise Miss, but I recently mislaid my watch. Heddsworth, can you assist?'

Heddsworth took out his fob watch and told Rose the time to the minute. 'A shame about your watch, Rawlings,' he said. 'Essential tool of the punctual butler.'

'Indeed, sir,' said Rawlings, clearing his throat. 'As I said, I am afraid I misplaced it.'

'Could it have been stolen?' asked Rose. 'There are so many pickpockets around Yorke.' She shuddered, the picture of a protected young lady afraid of common criminals. 'They must be a great worry for the mayor.'

Rawlings linked his gloved fingers together. 'Perhaps it was stolen, miss. But I wouldn't know about the mayor's concerns. My role is to run his household and lighten the load. He has a great deal on his mind, with the railways to run.'

'Yes, not to mention this dog attack in the Shudders,' said Rose guilelessly. 'Frightfully scary. I have a mind to avoid the place entirely until the dog is captured. Do you ever visit the Shudders, Mr Rawlings? It can't be safe at night any more.'

Rawlings' huge hands curled. 'I don't go there at night, miss, no.'

He's lying! Rose thought. Moll the Pocket only went to the skitterways at night – and if she'd robbed Rawlings he must have been there at least once. What was he hiding?

The Lord Mayor turned to greet them. Rose had

seen him before, at the opening of official buildings and at garden parties. Tall and slightly stout around the stomach, he looked impatient with the notion of sitting still in a church when there was work to be done. He was a man with a wide forehead and a bulldog jowl that even a beard could not conceal. Rose thought he looked tense and distracted, but then he did have the matter of the dog attack to deal with.

'Sir,' said Rawlings, 'have you met Miss Rose Raventhorpe? This is her friend Orpheus and her butler Heddsworth.'

'Ah. His Lordship's daughter.' The mayor's voice was deep and gruff. 'A good ambassador, Lord Frederick. If rather too opinionated about my railway empire. Remarkably forceful terms he uses for a peer of the realm. How do you do, Miss Raventhorpe? A question about my railways, was it?'

'Actually I have concerns about the Wakemen,' said Rose. 'Orpheus and I met some on the walls. I'm afraid they were terribly insolent.'

'More than insolent,' said Orpheus coldly.

'Up on the walls, were you?' The mayor exuded disapproval. 'Two children alone? Miss, do you understand the danger of gadding about the city, especially right now? A woman has been killed by a savage dog. I didn't hire the Wakemen for their manners. They're to keep the peace and find that beast.'

'Sir, if I may be so bold,' began Heddsworth, 'they do not seem to be helping the situation.'

The mayor grunted. 'That is a bold statement, sir. I don't like being questioned on my decisions. I know your father allows you a great deal of freedom, Miss Raventhorpe, but I suggest that a young lady's place is at home with her family, not interfering with city matters.'

Heddsworth's hand tightened on his walking stick. Rose bristled at the rebuke, but before she could speak the mayor consulted his pocket watch. 'Time to go, Rawlings. I have business appointments. Good morning to you all.' He nodded to them and left.

'Careful, Rose,' Orpheus whispered. 'You've got a glare that's going to stay on the mayor's back for days.'

Rose laughed despite herself. 'He didn't have to be so – cloddish,' she complained. 'And Rawlings was lying about never visiting the skitterways. Why?'

'He may have had any number of reasons,' Heddsworth pointed out. 'Come along, we should go home for lunch.'

'I'd rather go for a walk first,' said Rose. 'We've been sitting in that cathedral too long. You take the carriage home, Heddsworth, and we'll walk.'

'By yourselves?'

'It's a lovely day,' said Rose.

Heddsworth narrowed his eyes at her.

'Oh fine, I want to go back to Mad Meg Lane,' Rose admitted. 'Perhaps there is some clue there that we missed while the police were there. It would be easier to investigate without them around.'

'A good idea,' said Heddsworth. 'But be careful, please.'

Orpheus patted his chest. 'I'll look after her,' he said. Rose pulled a face at him.

'You must take a cab home afterwards,' Heddsworth warned them. 'Or the Stairs Below. Understand?'

'Yes, Heddsworth,' they chorused. He climbed into the carriage and ordered the driver back to Lambsgate.

The Shudders was only a short stroll from Cathedral Green. Out of long habit Rose looked up at the cat statues they passed on the way. The sight always comforted her. Nothing could go truly wrong in Yorke while they stood guard.

Yet she hesitated at the entrance to the skitterway. That awful, inexplicable feeling of dread came again.

'Enough!' she muttered to herself, walking down the dark alley with Orpheus close behind. 'It's just a skitterway. There's only rubbish down here, and dirty puddles and—'

She stopped as if someone had slapped her.

A huge, dead black mastiff lay on the ground. It had been shot in the head.

Chapter 6

Blood in the Skitterway

Rose dropped to her knees beside the corpse. As she knelt by the dog, a woman came hurrying down the skitterway with a shopping basket. When she saw the scene in front of her she screamed and dropped her basket. People came running, and a crowd began to build.

'Has it struck again?'

'Is the girl hurt?'

'Mercy, is it dead? Looks terrible savage!'

Rose's heart was still trying to hammer

through her ribcage. She examined the corpse.

It wasn't Wolf. It didn't look at all familiar. She forced herself to touch the dead creature. It was stone cold.

She studied the size of the corpse. It had been a big dog. Almost monstrous. But thin – its ribs showed, and there were mangy patches on its back.

The crowd muttered. 'Looks a bad 'un,' she heard one man say. 'Poor Moll didn't stand a chance against that.'

'Good riddance to the thing.'

'Hope it's buried out of the city. What if its ghost roams in the night? I ain't goin' near this place in the dark.'

'Shh! It's bad luck to speak of the Barghest.'

Then Rose heard deep triumphant laughter.

'Here is the beast, dead as a nail!' shouted Bathory the Wakeman. He strode up, his cloak swirling around him. He smirked at Rose. 'What do you think, miss? A pretty sight? Shot it myself, I did.'

'What the blazes are you playing at, Bathory?' snarled Orpheus. 'There wasn't a soul in this alley when we found the dog.'

'I was checking that nobody in the area had been harmed by the creature,' said Bathory. 'You're very lucky you weren't here at the time – the dog could have attacked you!'

The crowd was thick now, but Bathory flourished his pistol. 'Yes, I shot this infernal creature!' he shouted. 'It came upon me just now with slavering jaws. But I held steady and fired. My bullet sank into its skull. The reign of terror is at an end, people of Yorke. You may go about your business in safety, while we patrol and keep such beasts at bay!'

'Shot it?' muttered Orpheus. 'I didn't hear a shot. It looks like the thing's been dead for hours.'

The crowd did not disperse in a hurry. People wanted to get a closer look at the dog. Bathory's triumphant smile faded as Rose continued to inspect the body. 'What kind of morbid child are you? We need to move this corpse before it stinks up the whole lane.'

Ignoring him, Rose inspected the dog's paws. The forepaws were big, but Rose felt sure that the print she had seen on the cobbles was bigger still. She covered her fingers with a handkerchief and lifted the dog's upper lip to inspect its fangs.

'The teeth are all worn down!' she exclaimed. 'And the muzzle here – it's grey.' She touched it with the handkerchief, and black soot came away on the fabric.

'You leave that!' Bathory darted forward. 'Don't touch it. This thing is evidence.'

'Evidence?' snapped Rose. 'Evidence of trickery, most likely. Why is the dog all sooty? To hide its age?'

'Its back leg was broken once,' Orpheus added, pointing to an ill-healed injury. 'The poor thing wouldn't be able to run faster than a limp. And you call yourself brave?'

'That "poor thing" was a killer!' Bathory waved his pistol. 'Back now, all of you. Wakemen's orders.'

'I don't believe this dog attacked anything!' Rose argued. 'If anyone has been mucking with corpses, it's you!'

Then someone rushed past her and knelt beside Rose to bend over the corpse. It was Miss Wildcliffe. 'Who shot this poor brute?' she demanded. 'You, Bathory? Why? Did it make the mistake of breathing on you?'

Bathory folded his arms. 'Well, well – the Moorland Witch! Was this a friend of yours?' He kicked the corpse. 'Went for my throat, it did. Got it just in time.'

'I suppose the poor creature didn't pay you a fine,' Miss Wildcliffe retorted. 'Well, I won't pay you protection money, and I hope nobody else has, either!'

Rose scanned the crowd. Some people looked embarrassed, as if they had indeed been forced to pay fines to the Wakemen. But some cast sidling looks at Miss Wildcliffe.

'The Barghest is summoned by a witch,' someone muttered. 'And she was seen in Mad Meg Lane the morning after the attack. The Wakemen ought to arrest her before she raises that dead hound again.'

'She's the one who writes of the Barghest,' added a man. 'The Moorland Witch. She could have called up its evil spirit in the first place.'

The authoress sighed. 'So now it is my doing? I did not call up the Barghest. My dog hurt nobody. It's complete nonsense.'

Orpheus tugged Rose up by the elbow. 'We'd better go home,' he said. 'Heddsworth and the other butlers will want to hear about this.'

Bathory overheard him. 'Butlers?' he said. 'My Wakemen have met some of them. Very high and mighty, the butlers in this city. Some even carry weapons! Got ideas above their stations. Living in a fancy Hall like the gentry! That sort of place should belong to the real defenders.' He lifted his voice. 'The Wakemen are the true defenders of Yorke!'

People cheered. Rose reluctantly left Mad Meg Lane. Her last view of it featured Bathory posing like Saint George slaying a dragon. 'The beast has been caught,' he boasted. 'Everyone can sleep soundly tonight!'

Rose did not sleep soundly that night. She dreamt of entering a shadowy skitterway with Watchful the cat at her side. The ghost of Mad Meg appeared, a look of dread on her transparent face. 'The demon hound,' whispered Mad Meg. 'He's back. He's back. The Guardians must fight him. Can you not help, miss?' Then there were glowing red eyes and a horrible howling. Rose jerked awake, pinned to the bed with terror, and was unable to go back to sleep.

People had seemed much happier in the streets the day before, jubilant that the Barghest had been caught. But Rose was uneasy, especially with the Wakemen strutting about as if they owned the city.

She made herself get up and dressed, ringing for Agnes to help her do her hair and prepare for breakfast. She wondered if there was any mail for her. Lady Constance would most likely have sent a note from London, expressing her hope that Rose was taking her piano and dancing lessons.

Heddsworth's voice came urgently from behind the door. 'Miss Raventhorpe, are you awake? Dressed?'

'Yes, why?'

'I'm afraid there has been another incident in Mad Meg Lane. The grocery boy heard the news. There was blood on the cobblestones and Sergeant Snodgrass was called. Apparently, he is most upset this has happened again. And at the stroke of midnight! I'm beginning to think he believes there must be a supernatural hound involved.'

Rose's appetite for breakfast vanished. She threw on her coat and a hat and hurried to join Heddsworth, leaving Agnes protesting.

Heddsworth followed Rose downstairs. They set out into the chilly dawn, hailing a hansom cab to take them to the Shudders.

At this time of day, the Shudders was quiet. Shops were just starting to open, and staff were sweeping floors and washing windows. People stood in huddles, talking in low, anxious voices. A haggard-faced Sergeant Snodgrass was there, snapping orders to several constables. Constable Murton was among them, looking extremely shaken. 'The dog may still be about,' Rose heard the sergeant say. 'Keep searching! We'll have the Wakemen to answer to if we don't succeed!'

Rose and Heddsworth exchanged looks, and sneaked past the sergeant into the skitterway. Rose felt guilty – the poor sergeant was doing his best, and they would be in significant trouble if he caught them. But she had to see what had happened in Mad Meg Lane.

They found a trail of fresh blood on the

cobblestones, some distance from the place where they had found the dead dog, but there was no sign of a victim. Rose steeled herself. 'If someone was attacked, where are they now?'

The unpleasant question drove them further down the skitterway. There was no one to be seen. Rose peered at the cobbles, looking for blood spots.

She paused. The scent of chocolate wafted through the air.

'Heddsworth,' she said suddenly. 'The Chocolate Emporium should have a back door that opens on to this skitterway.'

Rose studied the buildings, went to a door and pushed.

The door eased part-way open. The chocolate smell grew stronger.

A crumpled, bloody figure lay face down on the floor. Rose had a brief, sickening memory from her past – the death of someone she had loved. She tried to force down her nausea.

Heddsworth touched the man's arm. 'Still alive,' he muttered. 'Barely.' He turned the man gently on to his back. Rose covered her mouth. The man's chest was a mess of long, bloody claw marks. But that was not the only shock. She recognised him.

It was Lord Mayor Edward Chesney.

'The Barghest leaves a wound that never heals.'

'It prowls the Shudders, looking for victims.'

'It appears when someone dies, and follows their funeral bier.'

'Nay, it warns of a death t' come!'

'It drags chains behind it at night. Ye can smell the sulphur.'

Yorke was a city on the edge, a seething cauldron of fear. The Lord Mayor himself had been attacked and left for dead. People armed themselves with whatever weapons they could find. 'The Devil Hound's out! Stay in your homes at night! Bolt your doors!' they hissed to each other.

'Ought to brick up that skitterway. It's bad luck, that place. Cursed.'

'The mayor himself saw the red eyes. Then it struck him on the back like a hundredweight.'

Rose read articles in the Yorke newspapers, searching for the facts. They reported that the mayor lay in hospital, recovering slowly. He was not up to talking or seeing visitors. The Wakemen said they would patrol the city to find his 'vile attacker'.

'I thought this would at least stop the Wakemen,' Rose told Heddsworth, chin in hand. She was eating breakfast in the kitchen while Heddsworth polished the silver. 'They claimed that poor dead dog was the killer. Now the mayor has been attacked, proving them wrong, but they behave as if they own the city. They're still extorting money from people. I'm afraid they are going to blame Miss Wildcliffe.'

'I agree,' said Heddsworth, pouring tea into a porcelain cup. 'And I would like to know why the mayor was in the skitterway in the middle of the night. Rawlings might know, but he doesn't seem inclined to tell us. And we still haven't located the savage dog.' He paused. 'There is something else odd, now that I think of it. Dogs bite when they attack – they don't use their claws. But the victims found in Mad Meg Lane were both clawed at.'

Rose nodded thoughtfully. 'A huge dog that no one has properly seen, that left one pawprint, and claws its victims instead of biting them. Why has no one seen it? Why is it only attacking people in the middle of the night? That doesn't sound like an ordinary dog to me.'

Heddsworth picked up his tin of silver polish. 'Then what, Miss Raventhorpe, do you think is at work here? A real person deliberately setting a dog on its victims?'

'No,' said Rose at last. 'I thought Rawlings might have done that, but now I'm not so sure. I mean, if you want to hurt or kill people, why go to the trouble of taking a fierce hound to a skitterway? It's risky, isn't it? A savage dog wouldn't be easy to control, or to hide. Why wouldn't you simply do the job yourself?' She paused.

'You mean—' began Heddsworth.

Rose pushed her boiled egg aside, her eyes alight with eagerness. 'What if it wasn't a dog at all? That was what we all assumed. But it could be a person. Someone pretending to be the Barghest. Hiding behind the legend.'

Heddsworth set the tin down and stared into space. 'Saint Iphigenia's cats,' he murmured. 'That would fit. Nobody has seen the dog because there isn't one.'

Rose nodded avidly. 'Moll the Pocket was supposedly scratched with sharp claws. That could be done with a sharp implement. That pawprint we saw would be easy to fake with some carved wood and blood from the butcher's. It seemed so – so staged, so obvious. Like something from one of Harry Dodge's theatricals.'

Heddsworth toyed with a well-polished fork. 'If

this is true, someone is going to a lot of trouble to attack people. We need to know the motive. Why was Moll murdered? Why was the mayor attacked? How could they be connected?'

'I thought Rawlings might be responsible for Moll's death,' Rose admitted. 'But you're right, it seems a lot of trouble to go to for the sake of a watch. Unless he only meant to confront her, and killed her by accident. He could have put the pawprint on the cobblestones to cover up his crime. What if the mayor realised that, and made it clear that he suspected him? Rawlings would have to kill the mayor too, to silence him.'

'I doubt he would attempt to murder two people, no matter now fond he was of his watch,' Heddsworth objected.

'Maybe not,' said Rose. She sighed. 'At least the mayor was not killed. When he recovers he might be able to tell us what happened.'

Heddsworth began to clear away the breakfast dishes. 'Shall we visit the chocolate emporium again? After all, we found the poor man there after the attack. The shop staff may have answers to some of these questions.'

Rose sat up with a jolt. She remembered Sylvia, Dr Jankers' niece. She had seemed intensely keen on publicity for the shop, even if it was the negative publicity of the dog attack. Rose had been disgusted by her attitude to Moll's death, but was there a more sinister reason behind it? The mayor had been found in the emporium. Could Sylvia be involved in the crime? Was she cold-blooded enough to commit murder?

Chapter 7

Blades in the Night

Rose and Heddsworth found a rather quiet and deserted chocolate emporium when they entered. Lorimer was sitting slumped at a table and a rather pale Sylvia was counting out the till.

Lorimer shuddered when Rose said they had come to ask him about the attack. 'It has been a terribly trying time,' he admitted. 'The papers have been full of it. I am simply grateful that our door was left open. If it was not for that, the mayor might have been killed by the Barghest.'

Sylvia looked irritated. 'It was careless of you to leave a door open, Lorimer. We could have been burgled.'

'Aren't you sorry the mayor was hurt?' Rose demanded. She felt like throwing a chocolate box at Sylvia. 'That open door saved his life.'

Sylvia reddened. 'Well, of course. But I thought – I thought everything would quieten down once that wretched dog was shot. I can't understand why the mayor has been attacked! The mayor! It makes no sense at all!'

'Nothing about these attacks makes sense,' said Rose. 'In fact I happen to think it wasn't a dog that attacked him after all. I believe that a pawprint I saw in the skitterway was faked, and someone is committing deliberate murder.'

The young woman gaped at her. 'Murder? But that's – that's impossible! It was a *dog*. It was good for business for a while, when people started repeating that silly story about the Barghest. But if it gets out that this was murder, people will be too frightened to come to the Shudders at all. We'll lose all our business.'

Rose thought Sylvia seemed genuinely shocked. If not, she was a good actress. Rose looked around. It was true that the shop looked quieter than usual. The Shudders, normally so bustling, felt neglected and forbidding to Rose. The shop doors were shut. Shop-owners had taken off on sudden holidays. Sylvia rubbed her hands against her apron, her face full of worry. Rose drew a deep breath.

'Can you think of anyone who might be responsible for the attacks?' she asked.

Sylvia looked away. 'I don't know. I have seen Batty Annie around here. She's been selling talismans to ward against the Barghest. Don't you think that's strange? Lorimer has half a dozen of them.'

Rose was discomfited. She had never once suspected Batty Annie. But then – what if Batty Annie had secretly loathed her niece, and done away with her?

'I don't believe in witches, but she's creepy,' Sylvia whispered. 'The way she stares at you, as if she knows all your secrets.'

Rose had felt that look herself. Now she wondered what kind of secrets Sylvia had. Why was she so anxious? Was she perhaps a thief? Stealing from the shop till?

'You're not in any kind of trouble are you, Sylvia?' she asked gently. 'You seem very tense.'

'I'm not tense!' snapped Sylvia. 'And there's nothing wrong, apart from this terrible attack being bad for business. I want to make a success of this place. I need to show my uncle that I'm a responsible, capable person. Now you must excuse me, I have orders to fill and chocolates to make.'

And she marched off, her starched hair-bow as rigid as her back.

Rose stood watching her, thinking. Sylvia's manner seemed guilty – but of what?

Just then, the bullying voice of Bathory was

heard in the skitterway. Rose and Heddsworth looked at each other in dismay, and left the door of the emporium.

Rose, Orpheus and Heddsworth found the Wakeman interrogating a man Rose recognised as Flinty the Forger. A thin, weak-chinned, shabbily dressed man, Flinty made his living faking antiques. He hugged his antiquities to his chest as the Wakeman shouted at him.

"You're a lying pest and a conman and a nuisance! We're in charge while the mayor is out of action, and we say you're to leave Yorke for good. There's plenty of criminals and no-accounts who don't deserve to live within these walls.'

'But I got to earn a living,' Flinty protested. 'Look, I've some excellent bargains here. Genuine Roman artefacts. You can have 'em for a song.' He held out some glazed stone pots.

'I don't want that rubbish!' Bathory hurled them into the gutter.

Rose was not over-fond of Flinty, but that was

too much. 'Stop that at once!' she shouted. 'Leave him alone!'

'Oh, it's dear little Miss Raventhorpe again. Why don't you go back to your nursemaid?' drawled Bathory. He waved his rapier at Flinty. 'Get moving, or I'll sign my name on your back.'

Flinty bolted.

'May I ask who else you are expelling from the city?' Heddsworth asked Bathory.

'Troublemakers, butler,' snapped the Wakeman. 'Troublemakers like the Raven Society, for one. That vagrant lot of chimney-sweeps.'

'There's nothing wrong with them!' Rose was indignant.

'Friends of yours, are they?' Bathory snorted. 'Not surprised. Nosy lot they are, with their filthy bird mascots. And they wouldn't pay us a penny to prove their honesty. Makes them criminal characters in my book.'

'Is this what the Lord Mayor wants?' asked Heddsworth.

'The Lord Mayor's laid up in hospital,' said Bathory smugly. He waved the rapier close to Heddsworth's face. 'For all we know he won't recover. So we're in charge now. Off you go. Serve your tea, polish your silver, whatever it is you do.'

There was a line of wet washing strung over Bathory's head. Swiftly, Heddsworth drew his rapier and sliced the line in half so that the washing fell on to the astonished Wakeman. Rose burst out laughing.

Clawing wet washing from his head, Bathory shot them a venomous glare. 'A butler with a sword,' he snarled. 'I won't stand for it. We're the real defenders of Yorke, understand?'

Heddsworth turned away. A window opened above them, and a woman began shouting at Bathory to pick up her laundry. Rose was delighted. But as she turned to go, she saw the look in Bathory's eyes as he stared after them. He would not forget that humiliation.

*

That night, Agnes the maid knocked on Rose's bedroom door.

'What is it?' Rose asked groggily.

'It's young Master Orpheus, miss,' whispered Agnes. 'Says there's trouble out in the city.'

Rose blinked, instantly awake. 'What kind of trouble?'

'The Wakemen, miss. They're attacking Silvercrest Hall.'

Rose dressed faster than she ever had in her life. She grabbed her rapier. Orpheus was waiting downstairs. 'I took Inaaya to the Dodges' house.' He pushed his hat down over his hair, and straightened his coat. 'I knew something bad was coming. Heddsworth's packing his medical kit.'

They hurried downstairs to the butler's pantry. 'I can't find Watchful,' Orpheus added. 'But that cat has a better sense of danger than I do. He'll look after himself.'

They found Heddsworth putting on his coat. 'What can you tell me, Orpheus?'

'One of the sweeps sent a raven with a message,' said Orpheus. 'The Wakemen have ordered the sweeps out of the city at swordpoint. Now they're coming after the butlers. Saying they're a danger to the city, or some such rubbish.'

Heddsworth nodded. 'I will go to the Hall now. You two must wait here.'

'No, we won't,' said Rose.

'We'll follow you,' said Orpheus.

'Out of the question,' said Heddsworth.

'Out of the window, more like,' said Orpheus. 'Come on, Heddsworth. You can't tell us to stay here while the Wakemen create havoc. The Hall is my home too.'

Heddsworth lifted the window sash. 'I'm sorry, but this time you must stay here. I don't know what those Wakemen will do.'

And he climbed out the window, shutting it firmly behind him.

Rose and Orpheus looked at each other.

'What do we do?' asked Orpheus.

'We need a lantern,' said Rose. 'We're taking the Stairs Below.'

The city was quiet, but a soft wind tousled the trees, and the stars were obscured by clouds. A moonless night; a good night for dark deeds.

They reached a door to the Stairs Below – a small, ordinary-looking one set in a stretch of brick wall. Orpheus fished his Infinity Key from its chain, and turned it in the lock. The tiny key opened the door, and they stepped inside.

Silence. Rose had half-expected to hear the shouts and clashes of a battle.

Orpheus held up the lantern while they walked in the direction of the Hall.

'What if we meet someone?' Orpheus muttered.

'That depends on who it is,' said Rose. 'If it's a Wakeman, we'll have to fight or run. Hopefully they won't have found out about the Stairs Below.'

'But what if they have? What if they've hurt

someone?' Orpheus continued. 'I mean – what if we find a body in here?'

'Orpheus!'

'Well, we might.'

Rose swallowed hard. There were rats in the Stairs Below. If they found a body – no, she wouldn't think about it.

They hurried on, passing more doors. Rose unlocked one or two, just to see what was happening out in the city. Each time they saw nothing amiss. Gas-lights flared. Rats scurried. As they walked, Rose counted doors. The next door would be on Ravensgate, and then came the one that led to Silvercrest Hall.

Rose stopped so suddenly Orpheus cannoned into her.

'What the—?'

The door to the Hall, tall and ancient, was carved with Latin words. *Et gladio et polies.* With sword and polish. Someone had broken it down. It looked like they had used an axe.

The lantern trembled in Rose's hand. She drew her rapier. Orpheus guarded them from behind. They stepped over the threshold.

The doorway led into the ballroom of the Hall, which typically dazzled with mirrors and chandeliers. Now the floor was a mess of broken statuary. Mirrors had been smashed. Silver cutlery lay scattered across the round table.

'Where is everyone?' whispered Orpheus.

They heard footsteps approaching the other door of the ballroom. Rose almost sprinted back to the Stairs Below. Resolutely she held her ground, her heartbeat arguing loudly in her ears.

A dishevelled Bronson, rapier in hand, ran in. She skidded to a stop in front of Rose and Orpheus.

'What are you two doing here?'

'We – we came to—' Rose stared at the mess all around them. 'What happened?'

'The Wakemen! They're all over the Hall,' said Bronson. 'At least twenty of them. They think this place is theirs now. Demanded we leave quietly, saying we were dangerous agitators. We chased most of them upstairs, but they're driving us back. Charlie wounded one, but—'

They heard a crash above them.

'Oh blast,' said Bronson.

More footsteps sounded, and Bronson whirled around. About ten trainee butlers stormed down the stairs. Among them was Miss Regemont, wearing a purple brocade dressing-gown, and carrying her own rapier. One arm was tied up with a piece of tablecloth. Red seeped through the fabric.

'They fight with no honour at all,' she informed Bronson crossly. 'When the Lord Mayor recovers I shall have words with him, I assure you!' She spotted Rose and Orpheus. 'Oh, for heaven's sake! This is no place for children!'

'We wanted to help!' said Orpheus. 'How bad is your arm?'

'It'll need stitches,' said Miss Regemont. 'I

had a duel with that wretched Bathory. Where's Heddsworth?'

Charlie Malone limped across the floor, as the other butlers took up defence positions around the stairway. 'On his way, madam – we've been holding them off in the fencing salon but we won't be able to keep them at bay for much longer. We need to regroup. Are we retreating, madam?'

'There's more of them than we thought.' Miss Regemont bit her lip hard. 'We'll have to.'

Shouts echoed from upstairs. Footsteps sounded on the stairwell. The butlers waited with swords drawn, but lowered them as Heddsworth appeared in the doorway, his knuckles bleeding through his white gloves. 'I'm afraid I was forced to strike one on the nose,' he told his friends. Then he spotted the children. 'Saint Iphigenia's cats! What did I tell you two? What will his Lordship say?'

'TEA TRAY!' shouted Rose.

Heddsworth ducked just in time to avoid a silver tray crashing into his skull. Glyde had thrown it from the stairwell. The Wakeman glared at Rose. Then a dozen Wakemen came rushing down the stairs behind him, and the battle was on again.

The butlers fought furiously. Rose pelted the Wakemen with forks and salt-shakers. Orpheus wielded the tea tray.

The Wakemen were winning by sheer force of numbers. 'Retreat!' Miss Regemont shouted.

Heddsworth practically threw Rose and Orpheus through the broken doorway to the Stairs Below. Then they were running down the network of passageways. They heard shouts behind them, but there was no sound of pursuing footsteps. The tunnel was so dark that Miss Regemont called 'Halt!' and everyone gathered in a panting group.

Rose heard the sound of a match being struck and Bronson's face appeared above the flame. 'Who's here?' she demanded. 'Anyone missing?' There was a quick roll call. All the butlers were accounted for.

'Any injuries?'

'Miss Regemont,' said Charlie. 'Pass the brandy.'

'I am not faint,' said Miss Regemont, wobbling. Heddsworth and Bronson supported her. 'Lean on us, madam. Here, some brandy,' said Heddsworth. 'Have you a candle, Mr Malone?'

Charlie found a candle in a coat pocket. Bronson lit it and they set off down the cold passageway. They came to a door at last, and Rose opened it with the key from her cameo. They stepped cautiously out. The street was peaceful. Nobody would guess at the chaos that had erupted at the Hall.

'So now they have Silvercrest Hall,' said Orpheus bitterly. 'Can we get it back? Make another attack?'

'That may have to wait,' said Miss Regemont. 'They gave me this.' She fumbled in a pocket and brought out a piece of paper, a large, official-looking document, bearing the mayor's seal.

The butlers of Silvercrest Hall are hereby evicted from the Hall and banned from the city of Yorke. If any butler resident of the Hall, or associate of the Hall, is seen within the walls of the city he will be sent to Yorke Prison. By order of the Wakemen, acting for the Lord Mayor of Yorke.

Chapter 8

Withering Downs

'But where are we going to go?' whimpered a butler.

The former Hall residents, mostly young students, staff and a few retired butlers, had gathered at Emily and Harry Dodge's house. The Dodges hurried back and forth with brandy, cups of tea and cake. Their eternally gloomy butler, Spillwell, provided bandages. He looked even more downcast than usual.

'They can't make you leave!' Rose was furious.

'She's right – they can't get rid of you!' said Orpheus. 'It was bad enough sending the sweeps away.'

'It seems we shall have to go,' said Miss Regemont. She looked pale and tired, reposing in an armchair after Bronson, who was most skilled at medical procedures, had stitched her arm. 'All of us.'

'And let those Wakemen take over the Hall?' Bronson looked ready to spit.

'Imagine the state the silver will get into,' groaned Miss Regemont.

'But you're homeless!' cried Rose. 'All of you! How many butlers are there at the Hall?'

'About twenty at present,' said Heddsworth. 'But it's not just the butlers living at the Hall that will have to leave. The Wakemen are acting as governor of the city in the mayor's absence – and according to their order anyone they associate with the Hall is banned. It would be easy for them to throw us all into prison if we acted against the order. They certainly won't tolerate the sight of me in Yorke.'

'I'm afraid you can't all stay here,' said Emily regretfully, wrapping a shawl around her growing belly. 'The house isn't big enough.'

'We shall not intrude on your family, Mrs Dodge,' said Miss Regemont. 'It is not to be thought of. Besides, the wretched Wakemen will find out, and then you will be in danger too.'

'We'll find somewhere,' said Charlie Malone, eating a scone. 'How about Italy? Sunshine and flowers. Excellent place to be exiled.'

'Delightful as that would be,' said Miss Regemont, 'the idea presents difficulties. We have few funds at our immediate disposal. And we must stay near Yorke. We are Guardians, and we will not abandon the city we protect.'

'Are all the butlers who ever studied at Silvercrest Hall banned?' Emily looked anxiously at her husband, an ex-butler.

'I don't think so,' said Rose comfortingly.

'I can help fix hurts,' piped up Orpheus's sister Inaaya. Once near-starved, she now had round dimpled cheeks, and hair prettily dressed with red ribbons. She wore a medical kit at her belt like the butlers. She had been greatly interested in Bronson's work as she stitched Miss Regemont's arm. Now she inspected Rose's hair, tutted, and brushed it into order.

'I know where you can go!' said Emily suddenly. 'Miss Wildcliffe has a huge old place out on the moors! It's a proper castle, called Withering Downs.'

'Would she let everyone stay?' asked Rose doubtfully. 'I don't want to get her into trouble. What if the Wakemen find out?'

'She lives beyond the city gates,' said Emily. 'And she hates the Wakemen; of course she will let you all stay. I will come with you, in our own carriage, and explain it all.'

'But we must leave the city as soon as possible,' said Miss Regemont. 'Otherwise those wretched

Wakemen will haul us off to prison. There is no time to send word to Miss Wildcliffe and we can't simply appear on her doorstep.'

'These are extraordinary circumstances,' declared Emily. 'You can all sleep here for the rest of the night, and leave first thing in the morning.'

The butlers looked relieved. Inaaya and Harry dug out pillows, blankets and cushions, while Spillwell arranged sofas and spare mattresses. Everyone was soon settled in some form of bed. Rose, now stumbling with tiredness, had to return home to Lambsgate with Heddsworth.

'I want to come with you all,' Rose told Heddsworth as they reached the front door. 'But what if Mother writes, or comes back from London?'

'We shall say you needed fresh air, and are having a nice walk in the moors. That will be true enough. Now off to bed – we both need some rest.'

Rose was very glad to go upstairs. Watchful

curled up on the covers as she plummeted into bed.

'Where were you tonight?' Rose asked. 'The butlers needed you!'

The cat only twitched his tail.

'Well, you can stay here and guard the city,' mumbled Rose sleepily. 'Because as of tomorrow, the human Guardians of Yorke won't be here.'

Watchful woke her at dawn the next morning. He rubbed his nose and whiskers against her face, startling her into consciousness.

Agnes was lighting the fire. Rose sat up.

'I've packed up a bag for you, miss,' Agnes whispered. 'Mr 'Eddsworth's takin' you for a walking holiday, 'e said.'

'On the moors, yes,' said Rose, struggling out of bed. She pushed at the velvet curtains and peered out the window. Pale spring sunlight washed over Lambsgate. She made a mental note to pack her rapier.

'I'll put in a good packed lunch for the journey,'

added Agnes. 'Mrs Standish made some for you all.'

When Rose went downstairs she found a picnic hamper waiting in the kitchen. It contained gingerbread, pork pies, bread and butter, Scotch eggs, lavender lemonade, sausage rolls, apples, cucumber sandwiches and crystallised violets.

Heddsworth appeared, carrying a flask of hot tea. 'Ah, good morning, Miss Raventhorpe. Jeremiah is hitching up the horses. We shall pick young Orpheus up at the Dodges' home.'

They made good time to Vicarsgate. Orpheus appeared, looking as bleary as Rose felt.

'Emily's waiting in her own carriage,' said Orpheus. 'She sounds keen to see Miss Wildcliffe again. Kept reciting her poetry at us this morning.'

As they rode through the streets, Rose peered out, looking for the cat statues. It was reassuring to see them. But once they had passed under Grimsgate Bar, the grand entrance to the city, her heart fell. She felt like a traitor, leaving Yorke.

They rode down the street, and out into the barer, wilder country of Yorkesborough. Daffodils were in bloom, and the sweeping stretches of heather gladdened the eye. Rose saw small villages, roaming sheep and ancient drystone walls.

Orpheus opened the picnic hamper and they ate an early breakfast. The carriage rolled down increasingly narrow and stony roads, until there was little more than a path.

The Dodges' carriage rolled up and managed to draw level with them. Emily's face appeared at the window. 'Isn't this a gorgeous, melancholy place?' she cried. 'A perfect home for lost souls and unquiet spirits!'

'Um, yes,' said Rose. 'It's very early – will you go ahead and tell Miss Wildcliffe about the ban? Before we all arrive at once? She must be a busy woman.'

'Of course!' said Emily. 'She has stock to feed, and poetry to write, and weather to record. Follow my carriage!'

'I doubt the carriages can go much further,' observed Heddsworth. They were jolted by the stony path, and the wheels caught in ruts. Thunder rumbled in the sky. Orpheus turned up the collar of his cloak.

'Saint Iphigenia's cats!' said Rose, looking at the darkening sky in alarm.

Heddsworth patted his coat. 'I have brought an umbrella, Miss Raventhorpe.'

As they rattled over a hill they saw a woman trudging towards them in the now-mizzling rain.

'Oh dear,' said Rose. 'She's getting soaked. Shall we ask her to ride with us?'

'I think she doesn't mind the rain,' said Heddsworth. 'That's Miss Wildcliffe and her dog.'

Emily's carriage was already slowing. Miss Wildcliffe glared fiercely at them. Wolf barked.

'Clear off!' shouted the woman. 'This is a private road!'

Emily waved. 'It's us!' she cried. 'You remember me, don't you, Miss Wildcliffe?'

Miss Wildcliffe scowled. 'All too well, from your last visit. What are you doing out here? Lost?'

Rose stuck her head out the window.

'I'm sorry for the unexpected visit,' Emily was saying. 'But we have a group of refugee butlers in desperate need of sanctuary. Withering Downs would be the perfect place for them.'

'Refugee butlers?' spluttered Miss Wildcliffe. 'What do you mean?'

'The Wakemen brutally drove them out of their home at Silvercrest Hall and have exiled them from Yorke. It is a complete injustice. You are strongly against injustice, aren't you, Miss Wildcliffe?' Emily beckoned to her friends. 'You've met Rose and Orpheus and Heddsworth.'

Mindful of the dog, the others climbed out of their carriage. Miss Wildcliffe studied them.

'How many people am I providing sanctuary for?' she asked suspiciously.

'Ah,' said Rose. 'Erm – perhaps a dozen.'

'A *dozen*? Where am I to put them all?'

'They are very self-sufficient,' Rose assured her. 'We can put them up in stables and spare rooms.'

'The spare rooms are falling apart.'

'The butlers can fix them! They're good at such things, aren't you, Heddsworth?'

'Well, elementary carpentry is not our specialty – but we can learn,' said Heddsworth.

'But – but what are they going to eat? My cow?' spluttered Miss Wildcliffe.

Heddsworth smiled. 'I am sure we can milk your cow, and perhaps there are villages nearby where we can purchase victuals?'

'You'd need a big village,' said Miss Wildcliffe, arms crossed. 'And you are not slaughtering my pig.'

'Madam, we have no intention of harming your stock,' protested Heddsworth. 'It is an imposition, I know. We shall of course be giving you payment.'

Miss Wildcliffe shook her head. 'I'm not running a boarding-house. I don't want money. How long are you all proposing to stay?'

'The butlers need to stay until they get their Hall back,' said Rose. 'Hopefully soon. The Lord Mayor might help us, once he is out of hospital.'

The rain began to fall harder. 'Oh, come on then,' said Miss Wildcliffe. 'Follow me back to my house. No, I don't need a ride, thank you. My feet are good enough.'

'Strange, isn't she?' said Orpheus, as they all climbed back to their seats.

'Yes, but good-hearted, I think,' said Heddsworth.

Orpheus stuck his head out the window. 'Look at that!' he cried.

They had arrived at Withering Downs, a tumbledown, ivy-covered castle with battlements and a turret. There was also a pig pen, a cow stall, and a pile of cow manure near a vegetable garden.

Emily squealed from her carriage window. 'How picturesque it is! Utterly magical!'

'It's freezing and the roof leaks,' said Miss Wildcliffe. 'But it's far enough away from people.'

'It's like a home for the fairies!' said Emily.

Miss Wildcliffe glared. 'Fairies are not mischievous sprites. They are fierce, heartless creatures, free to ride on the wind.'

'I do love how you talk, Miss Wildcliffe,' breathed Emily.

Miss Wildcliffe snorted. 'I talk as I feel. I tell the truth. I've no time for people lacking courage, spirit, or common sense. In fact, I prefer most animals to people.'

'I feel that way about my dog, Bertram the Second,' said Emily. 'He has a soul, I'm sure of it. Animals are exceptionally sensitive creatures.'

The reclusive authoress stomped around to the pig pen. 'I have chores to do,' she called to her guests. 'Go in and make yourselves a cup of tea. Put your feet up, Mrs Dodge. And don't touch my writing-desk.'

'Very good, madam,' said Heddsworth.

'Here come the others!' shouted Orpheus.

A wagon was rolling down the hill. Miss

Regemont rode on the seat, while Charlie Malone and Bronson walked in front, leading the horse. The wagon pulled to a stop. It carried a pile of straw, which moved as something shifted underneath it, and then a number of bedraggled butlers sat up, coughing and disgruntled. They had been hiding under the straw to prevent the Wakemen learning where they were headed. Now they climbed out of the wagon, shook loose straw from their clothing, picked daisies out of their hats and stared dubiously at their surroundings.

'I say,' murmured one, 'it's more rustic than I was expecting.'

Miss Regemont spotted the owner of Withering Downs. 'Ah, Miss Wildcliffe! We apologise for imposing on your kindness. We are short of funds at present, but I assure you any expenses will be met.'

Miss Wildcliffe pushed her red hair back. 'I am not used to visitors,' she retorted. 'If you wish to stay, you will have to work on the farm to earn your keep.'

'We could take to highway robbery,' suggested Charlie Malone.

'Very funny,' said Bronson. 'Farm work will do.'

'Ploughing and sheep-shearing?' Charlie grinned. 'I'm not sure how much help we'll be.'

Bronson put her hands on her hips. 'We are not above any job, especially not honest farm work.'

Rose watched a butler step into a cowpat. He paled in horror.

'Farming *is* honest work,' Charlie agreed. 'But not something we're particularly good at.'

Bronson pulled on a fresh pair of white gloves. 'We are excellent household organisers, Charlie. How hard can it possibly be?'

Chapter 9

Domestic Upheaval

The butlers streamed into Withering Downs. Old and young, stout and thin, they looked around the house and immediately began cleaning it. One started to make sandwiches. Miss Wildcliffe was not pleased.

'I like things tidy,' she said, 'but not this tidy!'

'Cup of tea, madam?'

'You are looking tired, madam. Perhaps a jam tart would help.'

'This teapot is dented,' complained another butler.

'That's my grandmother's teapot! Hands off!' Miss Wildcliffe snatched the teapot.

'We must replace this carpet,' said another butler in scandalised tones. 'Look at it! Threadbare!'

'Windows need cleaning,' said one.

'Butter needs churning.'

'Mattresses need mending.'

'Linen should be bleached.'

'Why can't I find the grape scissors?' demanded one butler. 'Are they being repaired?'

Outside, three butlers were scrubbing the pig. Rose and Orpheus tried to find enough cups for tea. Miss Wildcliffe and Wolf stalked around, looking shocked.

'Miss Wildcliffe,' puffed Charlie, lifting a huge cooking-pot over the fire, 'have you ever considered building an indoor privy?'

'Certainly not! If the weather is brisk, I use a chamber pot.'

'But what about baths?' protested an elderly butler. 'Have you only this old tin thing?'

'Yes,' said Miss Wildcliffe. 'But it takes a lot of work to fill it. I suggest you use the beck.'

'The *river*? Outdoors?' spluttered the butler. 'Have you no sense of decency?'

'You'd only be observed by the local animal species,' snapped Miss Wildcliffe. 'Birds. Mice. Hedgehogs.'

'Intolerable,' declared the butler. 'No species of animal will see me in the altogether. I shall take a sponge-bath in the evenings.'

Two butlers were doing the laundry, pegging out underclothes. Miss Wildcliffe turned a funny colour when she saw her drawers on the line.

'Well, I think you are all nicely established now,' said Emily, looking around. Beds had been created out of mattresses, cushions and spare sheets. Candlesticks had been polished, and morning tea prepared from goods in the larder. Bronson swept past with dusty wine bottles in her arms ('That cellar needs organisation,') and the dog was gnawing on a bone by the hearth ('Really, he should be kept out of doors, madam.') Rose polished the windows with a rag while Orpheus ironed a tablecloth.

'I have never had so many guests in my life,' said Miss Wildcliffe.

'Don't the local people come round to tea?' inquired Emily.

'No, they keep to themselves.'

'Oh, what a shame.'

'I like the people of the moors,' declared Miss Wildcliffe. 'They are rough and hardy, like the land itself.'

'I am one with the landscape, too,' Emily assured her. '"*My spirit roams the moor, and at such hours I flee my fleshly cage.*"'

'Yes, I can quote my own lines, thank you. Well since you are all so nicely established, as you put it, I shall get on with my writing.'

'Poetry?' said Emily eagerly.

'No, my weather diary.' Miss Wildcliffe took a book from her pocket. She gave it to Emily. Rose read a page over her shoulder.

Monday. Rain.
Tuesday. Heavy rain, high winds.
Wednesday. Increasingly windy rain.

'So it's fierce weather here,' said Rose.

'I only consider it fierce when the roof comes off,' said Miss Wildcliffe. She reclaimed her diary, sat on a faded chair by the window, took up a pen and turned her back to the company.

Three butlers came in to wash their hands, having dealt with the pig, who was now clean and shiny.

Heddsworth brought in a pile of freshly cut wood and wiped his hands. 'I think we are all settled,' he said, looking around. 'And now,' he continued, gesturing to Rose and Orpheus to come closer, 'perhaps we should discuss the matter of the Wakemen, not to mention our investigation into the attacks by the so-called Barghest. Would you care to join us, Miss Wildcliffe?' He pulled out chairs at the kitchen table.

'I would rather not,' said the authoress, writing in her weather diary.

The butlers were all summoned from their various tasks. Everyone sat down to listen while Miss Regemont served everyone tea.

'Now,' said Heddsworth, 'first things first. How are we going to get Silvercrest Hall back from the Wakemen? Do we wait until the mayor recovers and find out if he really endorses the ban? Or do we act now, and take the Hall back by force?'

'If we do it by force we need numbers,' said Miss Regemont. 'Support.' She mused. 'I shall write to the other Silvercrest Hall butlers who are working around the country, or abroad. But it will take time for them to get here, if they can come at all.'

'We can collect them in our hot-air balloon!' cried Emily. 'Well, Harry will fly it. He wouldn't let me in my condition.'

'That is very generous, Mrs Dodge,' said Miss

Regemont. 'I shall inform the butlers.' She paused. 'I only hope that the Wakemen authorised that ban without the mayor's permission. I do not wish to make our Guardianship public knowledge, but he may have to be informed that we are protectors, not troublemakers.'

Miss Wildcliffe turned in her seat. 'So this wasn't necessarily the mayor's doing?' she asked, sounding surprised.

'We can't be sure, but we're assuming not – the ban did not occur until after he was attacked,' said Heddsworth.

Miss Wildcliffe pushed her weather diary aside. 'The bullies,' she muttered. 'They're nothing but blackmailers. And shooting that poor innocent dog. The real beast is probably hidden away in some back-street.'

'But it might not have been a dog at all,' said Rose, leaping to her feet. 'If somebody wanted to murder Moll the Pocket – and perhaps the mayor too – a dog attack would be a good cover for them.

Don't you see? People would either assume it was a real dog – or even the Barghest, the corpse-hound. But a sharp implement could have done the work of claws.'

Miss Wildcliffe stared at her. 'Who would do such a vile thing? An escaped lunatic?'

'It could have been carefully planned,' said Rose. 'Moll was a thief. She stole from the mayor's butler, Rawlings, and it's possible he attacked her in revenge. If the mayor was suspicious, Rawlings could have tried to silence him.'

'Rawlings?' Miss Wildcliffe shook her head. 'I find that hard to believe.'

'So do I,' said Heddsworth.

'Well, I don't believe it's a spectral hound,' said Rose, sitting down again with a bump.

'How can you be sure?' demanded an elderly butler named Primm. 'Miss Wildcliffe wrote of the hound herself!'

Miss Wildcliffe flushed. 'That was fiction.'

''Tis an evil creature, and no one should scoff

at it,' Primm insisted. 'I've seen the Barghest! I was only a boy then, but it was real enough. A red-eyed beast, a hound of terror, in Mad Meg Lane. It's the sword of Sigandus we need, the sword that went missing and which can cut a hole through walls. It's the only thing that can kill the Barghest. The only thing that can send it back to the darkness!'

'The sword of Sigandus?' Miss Wildcliffe said.

'The sword that went missing centuries ago,' explained Emily. 'According to legend. It would be an excellent subject for a Gothic poem. It is meant to be hidden in a rock somewhere, within the sound of bells. Only a true defender of Yorke can draw it out.'

'And presumably give it a good polish,' added Charlie. 'Five hundred years in a rock? Imagine the tarnish.'

'I found the book that refers to Sigandus,' said Heddsworth. He opened the small trunk he had brought with him, and handed a book to Rose.

She looked at the cover – *Servants and Swordsmanship*. As she turned the gilt-edged pages she saw that one chapter listed historic swords. They all had impressive names, like Joyeuse, and Sword of the Heaven of the Clustering Clouds. She found a reference to Sigandus.

'It is four feet long, and has a gold crosspiece and the image of a rose on the pommel,' she read aloud.

'No wonder someone nicked it then,' said Orpheus.

'We don't know that it was stolen,' said Miss Regemont. 'Hidden away, more likely. We have a fine collection of swords from all over the world in the Hall. But nothing that could be described as Sigandus.'

'Where was it last seen?' Orpheus wanted to know.

Heddsworth took the book from Rose and riffled the pages. 'Let me see – ah, yes. The founder of Silvercrest Hall, Arlington, was presented with the sword by the king. Arlington was butler to the mayor at the time, Sir Robert Cawdon. The story goes that Sir Robert wanted the sword, and Arlington was forced to hide it in stone, near the sound of bells.'

'It could still be found,' said Rose. She was beginning to feel intrigued by this story. If some of the butlers truly believed in the sword's ability to destroy the Barghest, it would help their morale to have it back. The people of Yorke would believe in its powers too. She remembered Bathory's longing for the sword. Could he be lured out of the Hall by the chance to get his hands on it?

'The sword was lost long ago, Miss Raventhorpe,' said Heddsworth. 'It is difficult to solve a mystery that old. All the people involved are long dead.'

'That just makes it more challenging,' said Rose. Orpheus grinned at her.

'Can we stop talking about lost swords?' demanded Miss Regemont. 'We have more pressing matters at hand. The city needs us to protect it, not those dreadful corrupt Wakemen.

They're nothing but criminals themselves. I intend to send word to the other butlers around the country and abroad, and find out how many can help us.'

Rose scowled. How could they simply sit back and wait? The thought that the butlers would never get the Hall back was too awful to contemplate.

The butlers all began talking at once. Miss Wildcliffe suddenly tugged at her hair. 'I can't think in these conditions. I need to commune with Nature!'

And with that she stalked out into the moors.

With the house full of unwanted guests, Rose and Orpheus decided the tactful thing to do would be to return to Yorke. Jeremiah, their driver, had been enjoying a peaceful snooze, after eating the remains of the picnic hamper. He helped them into the carriage and started the horses.

'I feel bad for Miss Wildcliffe,' said Orpheus, leaning back on the seat. Rose nodded guiltily.

The authoress liked peaceful solitude, and now her home was full of worried butlers.

They rolled into the city and down towards the Shudders. Then Rose drew in a breath. 'Jeremiah! Stop, please!'

The driver obeyed swiftly. Rose was out of the carriage almost before it had stopped moving. She had seen a jagged hole in the glass window of the Locks and Clocks shop, which specialised in exceptional jewellery and timepieces. Orpheus and Rose hurried through the door, and found Mr Goldsmith, the owner, sweeping up broken glass.

'What happened, Mr Goldsmith?' Rose glanced around the shop. 'Did someone break in?'

'No, no,' said Mr Goldsmith. He smiled at her wanly, showing a gold tooth. 'I think people are just upset about the attacks in the skitterway.'

'But that has nothing to do with you,' said Rose, bewildered.

The eldest Goldsmith daughter, Garnet, appeared from the workshop. 'It does where some people are concerned,' she said bluntly. 'Some fools thought the dragon statue over our shop looked too much like the Barghest. Some urchins were trying to throw stones at it, but they didn't have the best aim. Little wretches.'

'Garnet!' snapped her father. 'This will all blow over. Kindly help me to restore the display.'

'Yes, Father.'

Rose could hardly believe it. 'How could people be so ridiculous? Don't they use their brains at all?'

'People rarely do when they're frightened,' said Garnet. 'It didn't help that we refused to pay the Wakemen's protection fund. Or that we're Jewish. We are different, and sometimes that is all people need to hate.'

Orpheus and Rose helped the Goldsmiths to tidy the shop. 'I shall have the window replaced soon,' said Mr Goldsmith. 'In the meantime we must look after the stock, and see nobody steals it.'

Rose seethed over their ill-treatment. She needed to find out who was behind those attacks.

Rawlings was still a suspect, but all she really had as evidence was his lying about being in the skitterway at night. Could he have been there the night Moll was murdered? Sylvia Prentiss had seemed deeply invested in the success of the chocolate shop. Could she have used the Barghest as a means to drum up business? Or been so afraid that Moll the Pocket was driving customers away, that she had been driven to murder? Then there was Sylvia's suggested suspect – Batty Annie. The Junkyard Queen seemed to genuinely believe in the Barghest, but was her talk and her selling of talismans all a ploy? Had she attacked her own niece – and, if so, why? Then again, perhaps the real culprits were the Wakemen. Rose could easily believe Bathory capable of murder. He wouldn't blink at killing a pickpocket, thereby starting a city-wide panic and earning himself a job. And the attack on the mayor had given him power over the whole city of Yorke. She needed to question him again. If she could only get into the Hall!

'Have you seen anything suspicious?' Rose asked the Goldsmiths. 'Or heard anything related to the attacks?'

Mr Goldsmith shook his head. 'I simply hope the attacks stop, Miss Raventhorpe. The whole city is festering with fear and superstition. Even the butlers have gone now. How much worse can it get?'

Rose and Orpheus left the shop in a downcast state. They had to do *something*, Rose thought. Mr Goldsmith was right. Things couldn't get any worse than they were now.

Then they saw Glyde the Wakeman striding towards them. He had his hand on his sword hilt, and his gaze was murderous.

Chapter 10

The Moorland Witch

Rose and Orpheus bolted. They dashed across busy streets, leaping over horse dung and dodging carriages. Rose longed to disappear into the Stairs Below. But with the Wakemen at the Hall they couldn't risk it.

She stole a look over her shoulder. Glyde was catching up. Rose felt a pang of fear. He wouldn't hurt them in broad daylight – would he?

Glyde was on their heels. He reached out and

grabbed Orpheus by the shoulder, wrestling him to a halt.

Let him go!' Rose screamed.

A dark shape leapt from nowhere, hackles raised, a fury in fur. Wolf landed in front of the Wakeman, snarling. Glyde gasped, released Orpheus, and drew his rapier.

'Wolf! Come by!' shouted a familiar voice. Skirts swished past Rose. 'Sir, I will thank you to lower your weapon.'

Rose and Orpheus stared, panting for breath. Miss Wildcliffe stood glaring at the Wakeman. Wolf had backed off Glyde, but his hackles were raised and he was snarling.

'That dog shouldn't be allowed in the city,' shouted Glyde, but Rose noticed he kept a safe distance from Wolf.

'I brought him for protection!' Miss Wildcliffe shouted back. 'And it seems I was wise to do so, with you wretches attacking the innocent.'

'You're a witch.'

'Excuse me.' Miss Wildcliffe sounded fierce and lofty. 'I am nothing of the sort. I am a writer. My magic is in pen and ink.'

'That dog's wild,' said Glyde. 'Look at the claws on it.'

'The dog is better behaved than you, I daresay.'

Glyde gave Miss Wildcliffe a look of pure hatred before turning on his heel and marching away.

Miss Wildcliffe patted her dog. 'Now,' she said, turning to the children, 'what are you two up to? Running around like street urchins! I am surprised at you, Miss Raventhorpe.'

Rose caught her breath. 'We've been investigating the attacks. Why are *you* here, Miss Wildcliffe?'

'I needed to get away from my home, which is overrun with butlers. There are lace doilies in the privy!'

Rose and Orpheus shared guilty looks. Rose hoped the butlers would soon have their home back. She saw more people scowling as they passed Miss Wildcliffe, and heard angry mutters of 'witch'. How long would it be before Miss Wildcliffe dared not enter the city at all?

Rose and Orpheus returned to Withering Downs the next day, taking Inaaya with them to see the butlers. It was a beautiful spring morning out on the moors, welcoming after the fog in the city. The older children were quiet, letting Inaaya chatter as they travelled. It gave Rose a chance to think about the murders. She was beginning to think Bathory might be her prime suspect. But if he was the murderer, how could she prove it?

As they climbed from the carriage at Withering Downs, a hawk sailed through the sky. Miss Wildcliffe was outside her home watching it soar through the blue. She smiled and held out her arm. The hawk landed on the thick wool of her coat, flapping his wings.

'Hello, Dauntless,' she said.

'Oooh,' said the children together. 'Can we pat him?'

'Her. If you move slowly,' said Miss Wildcliffe.

They all advanced and touched the soft feathers. It was like caressing thunder.

Miss Wildcliffe whistled to the hawk. Dauntless shot off into the air, making Rose's stomach swoop as she watched her.

Then they spotted Heddsworth and went over to say hello. He was chatting to some local farmers, who had clearly come to see the strange doings at Withering Downs.

'Yes, we are butlers, sir,' Heddsworth was saying. 'We are not accustomed to working in the fields or with livestock, but we are doing our best.'

The farmers exchanged amused looks. 'But what is it you butlers do?' asked one. 'Can ye cook?'

'We can,' said Heddsworth. 'But we mostly direct the other staff of a household, and keep it in order.'

'I've heard a right strange thing, sir,' said the younger farmer eagerly. 'That ye use weaponry. Swords and the like.'

'Yes, we do fence on occasion,' said Heddsworth. 'It is a gentlemanly sport.'

'I'd like to try it,' said the young farmer.

The others chuckled. 'Would ye now, Gowkins?'

'He'll be makin' butter curls soon. Milkin' the cows into crystal vases.'

'Aw, no harm in askin',' said Gowkins, turning red.

'Not at all,' agreed Heddsworth.

'Miss Wildcliffe's pig seems to be getting nice treatment,' sniggered another farmer.

'Quite,' said Miss Wildcliffe, walking up to them. 'Have you no work to be getting on with?'

The farmers grinned at each other, and ambled away.

Rose glimpsed a number of butlers at work outdoors. Already they were beginning to look a little rough around the edges. Their clothes were rumpled, their polished shoes had been replaced by heavy boots, and their white gloves abandoned altogether. Instead of silver polish, they smelled of cow manure and sheep's wool.

'I think I'm taking to the rustic life,' said Charlie Malone, chasing a piglet across the vegetable patch. An elderly butler wiped down a clutch of freshly-laid eggs. Then a wild-eyed Bronson appeared from the shed. 'Triplet lambs!' she said, waving her mucky arms. 'Triplets! What a job! You wouldn't believe how I got them out!'

Only Heddsworth still looked immaculate. He welcomed the children. 'We're making morning tea,' he told them. 'A stew and an apple pie. Come in when you're ready for some.' Inaaya grabbed his hand and nearly dragged him indoors. Orpheus followed with a grin.

Rose turned to Miss Wildcliffe. 'I'm sorry about all this,' she said. 'We didn't want to inconvenience you – we just couldn't think of another way.'

'Oh, I know,' grumbled the authoress. She started walking off towards the river. Rose followed, sitting by Miss Wildcliffe on the grassy bank by the water. The authoress took a stone from her pocket and turned it over in her fingers.

'What's that?' Rose inquired, sitting too.

'This?' Miss Wildcliffe closed her fingers around the stone. 'It's a hearting-stone, from a drystone wall.' She saw Rose's puzzled face. 'In the Puritan days, the time of Oliver Cromwell,' she explained, 'some excessively pious persons decided to destroy a henge on the moors not far from here, a stone circle called the Stone Crown. The ancient structure was broken apart, the stones shattered.'

'How despicable!'

'It was a travesty. But some of those stones were used to make repairs in the drystone walls of the moors. Some, I believe, went into the walls of Yorke.'

Rose bit her lip. 'Can the stones be returned to their places on the moors?'

'I fear that is all but impossible.' Miss Wildcliffe

sighed. 'My brother Brannion liked the place. It is half a mile from here, downstream of this river. We used to pretend it was a fairy haunt.' The authoress rubbed her forehead. 'When Brannion fell ill, he used to rave it about it in his delirium. He claimed – he claimed the Barghest was chasing him. If only he could reach the stone circle, he said, he would be safe. Then he died.' Miss Wildcliffe turned the stone over in her fingers. 'I never told him about these. I know when they are from the Stone Crown.' She hesitated. 'They feel different. And they . . . tell me things. I shouldn't tell you that. You would think me raving mad. In older days someone would have burned me at the stake. A real Moorland Witch.'

'I don't think you're mad,' said Rose. 'What do the stones say, exactly?'

Miss Wildcliffe looked reluctant. She closed her eyes. Rose waited.

The woman gave the stone in her hand to Rose. It looked like an ordinary shard of stone.

'Turn it over,' Miss Wildcliffe instructed.

Rose obeyed. There was a faint scratch on the stone, lines that looked human-made.

'Those are runes,' said Miss Wildcliffe. 'When I find the stones, there are no marks on them at all. But the runes appear if I ask the stones a question. Simple things. "Watch." "Listen." "Storm." Like a riddle. Always the way with warnings, isn't it? Never straightforward. Always up for interpretation.'

Rose grinned. 'No reminders to feed the cat or have a bath.' She paused. 'Could I ask the stones a question, do you think?'

Miss Wildcliffe glanced at her. 'Do you expect the stones to solve a mystery for you?' she asked sharply. 'Rather than rely on your own skill?'

'No.' Rose looped her arms around her knees. 'But I do like to ask questions, and I might as well ask the stones. They might give more truthful answers than human beings.'

That made Miss Wildcliffe laugh. 'Oh, very well.' She took the stone out again and held it in her fist. 'Ask.'

Taking a deep breath, Rose concentrated on the stone. 'Where is the sword of Sigandus?'

They both waited.

'I don't know how long it takes to give an answer,' said Miss Wildcliffe. 'I just give them a minute.' She uncurled her fingers.

Rose gasped. The runes had changed.

'What do they say?'

Miss Wildcliffe studied them. She traced the letters with a fingertip. 'No,' she muttered at last. 'No, that can't be right.'

'Pardon?'

With a sudden movement, the authoress raised her arm and threw the stone into the river.

'What are you doing?' Rose leapt to her feet, and rushed into the cold water past her knees. She bunched her skirts in one hand, desperately searching for the stone. Ah, there it was! She reached in, and pulled the stone out. The new runes remained etched on the stone.

'Why did you do that?' she shouted, turning to Miss Wildcliffe.

But Miss Wildcliffe was no longer there.

Rose walked back to Withering Downs with the stone in her pocket and a frown on her forehead. The butlers were cleaning and polishing and cooking, but without their usual enthusiasm. Even the pig looked muddy, though it still smelled of lavender.

Rose went upstairs, and found Miss Wildcliffe at her desk, staring moodily out the window at the moors. She turned to face Rose.

'I apologise for my temper,' said Miss Wildcliffe. 'I can usually face unpleasant facts.'

'What upset you so much?'

'The runes. They said "brother".'

'Oh,' said Rose. 'Meaning . . . *your* brother?'

'Brannion,' said Miss Wildcliffe. 'The one who died.'

'I'm sorry,' said Rose. She paused. 'Why would the stone refer to him?'

Miss Wildcliffe sighed. 'Because Brannion was obsessed with the sword.'

'The sword of Sigandus?'

'We knew the old rhyme,' Miss Wildcliffe explained. 'My sisters, Brannion and I liked to play at searching for it. For us girls it was just fun, but for Brannion it was a passion. When he grew older he failed at nearly everything he turned his hand to, and he kept on searching for the sword. Day and night. He seemed to think it would make everything better for him. Then he died. He was something of a wastrel, Miss Raventhorpe, and I fear that hastened his end. And now the runes say – you know. What they say. I don't know what it means. Perhaps . . . perhaps after all he found the sword and hid it. If so, I do not want to find out. He was weak, but I don't like to think of him as a thief.'

'So Brannion might have found it?' ventured

Rose. 'Perhaps he left some clue as to what happened to it. Did he live here at Withering Downs?'

'No, he lived in our parents' house in Yorke,' said Miss Wildcliffe. 'We cleared out his room after his death, but found nothing incriminating.'

'Do you have any keepsakes of his?'

'Some letters,' said Miss Wildcliffe. 'And his journal. I have read them, I confess, but they make very little sense.' She looked at Rose. 'You wish to read them too, don't you?'

'Well, yes,' said Rose awkwardly. 'If you would allow it.'

Miss Wildcliffe stood up, and stalked over to a trunk by her bookcase. She opened it and rummaged through the contents. After a silence, she drew out a book.

Rose took the journal. There were sketches, scribbled poetry and entries: '*The sword is not in the cathedral, and I fear someone else may find it before me. Then what shall I do when the Barghest comes for me? I must not rest. I see it in my dreams – the red eyes, the teeth like blades.* A pressed leaf had been glued to one page, a scrap of lace to another. The writing was forceful at the start, but as time passed in the records the entries grew more and more spidery. *I dream I am on the wall, and the Barghest is stalking me. If I could only find the sword! But I am weak now, and can barely move from my bed. My sisters tell me to rest. They do not listen, they will not believe me when I speak of the hound of death.* Another, later entry: *I know where it is! I must reach it before the hound comes for me.*

Rose's hands shook. Brannion had dreamed of the wall, and the Barghest. The same dream as her own. How was that possible? If he had found the sword, might he have lived?

She thought of Batty Annie's conviction that the Barghest was real. Perhaps there was some truth to the legend. She still believed that a real person had attacked Moll and the mayor, but that dream . . .

And the Stone Crown. The hearting-stone. The rune that had said 'brother' . . .

'What if,' asked Rose, 'Brannion wanted to be taken to the stone circle because the sword was there? What if he thought it would protect him from the Barghest?'

The authoress sat very still. 'The Stone Crown?' she murmured. 'There's no sword at that place. I've been there.'

'It might be buried,' Rose suggested. 'According to the story, Arlington hid it from the mayor who wrongfully wanted to keep it. Maybe Brannion worked out where it was, but by then he was too ill to go and find it. Maybe he tried and failed. We may never know.'

'Yes,' muttered Miss Wildcliffe. She sat very still. 'Perhaps I owe it to Brannion to search for it. Even if it is only a futile gesture.'

'I know it might be futile,' said Rose. 'I might be completely off the mark.'

'But if there was any chance—' Miss Wildcliffe

shot to her feet. 'Let us go to the Stone Crown then. And take some of your butler friends with us. I know the legend. Only a true defender of Yorke may retrieve the sword. If Brannion was right, we have to do this properly.'

Chapter 11

The Heart of the Stone Circle

Orpheus insisted on coming with them, as did Inaaya and several of the butlers. 'I want to take part in this quest,' said Bronson, shouldering a spade. 'Even if it's hare-brained.'

'I don't like disturbing a stone circle,' said Charlie quietly. 'It feels insulting to the fairies. I'm Irish on my father's side; I don't like upsetting the green folk.'

'We will offer them an apology in advance,' said Bronson, amused.

'Are we digging for gold?' asked Inaaya.

'Not quite,' said Orpheus. 'An old sword.'

'If we find any gold can we keep it?'

'Not if it's fairy gold,' said Heddsworth. Bronson muttered 'nonsense' under her breath.

They reached the stone circle before Charlie's bad leg grew too tired. The jagged remains of stone looked sad to Rose. If there were fairy folk, she thought, they would have been heartbroken about the destruction of their home.

Even Bronson was angry. 'What a mess!'

'So what do we do now?' Orpheus asked Miss Wildcliffe. 'Choose a spot and dig?' He paused uncertainly. Miss Wildcliffe looked uncomfortable.

'I really don't know. Perhaps we should start in the middle of the circle?'

'All right then,' said Orpheus, and stepped into the centre. 'Here.'

He began to dig. The others came to help,

carefully laying the turf aside so they could repair the damage. 'I feel like an archaeologist,' said Rose.

'I feel daft,' said Bronson. 'I'm glad I brought a flask of tea.'

'How deep you do suppose the sword would be buried?' asked Charlie.

'Hopefully not far,' said Miss Wildcliffe.

'I've hit something,' said Orpheus. Then, 'Oh, it's a rock. Never mind.'

After ten more minutes of digging, when Rose was near admitting defeat, Charlie Malone said, 'Look!'

Everyone stopped. Charlie swept dirt away from a jagged piece of ancient stone. Jutting out from the stone was a hilt.

'The sword?' whispered Miss Wildcliffe. 'Sigandus?'

'We'll see.' Charlie scraped at the soil with his hands. The hilt had a rose on its pommel. Rose nearly shrieked with excitement.

'How did it get into the stone?' Charlie was awed. 'How is that possible?'

'And who's going to get it out?' muttered Bronson.

'Ladies first?' suggested Heddsworth gallantly. 'Miss Regemont is the head of the Hall. Would you like to try, madam?'

'Very kind of you, Heddsworth,' said Miss Regemont, 'but I would rather let Bronson try first.'

Bronson flexed her fingers. 'I'm honoured, madam. Although I do feel slightly silly about this.' She knelt to inspect the rock and the sword itself. Then she took hold of the hilt, braced herself, and heaved upwards.

The sword did not budge.

Bronson let go with a gasp. 'Dratted thing is stuck fast! We'd be better off digging it out.'

'Can I try?' Orpheus was practically bursting out of his skin.

'Me!' shouted Inaaya. 'Let me!'

Smiling, Bronson stepped back to let them take their turn. Orpheus and Inaaya tried pulling the sword out together, then separately. 'It didn't work,' said Inaaya sadly. 'It's broken.'

'It was an excellent attempt,' said Charlie Malone. 'Shall I have a go?' He closed his eyes as he took hold of the sword. Rose crossed her fingers for him. But the sword stayed firmly where it was.

'Ah well,' said Charlie, stepping back. 'The fairy luck isn't with me today. I knew they weren't pleased about us digging.'

'Shall I try?' Rose had barely been able to restrain her eagerness. Everyone nodded.

She touched her cameo for luck. Then she wrapped her hands around the hilt. Like Charlie, she closed her eyes. She breathed the smells of the moor, and felt the breeze on her face. *Please*, she thought. *I'm a Raventhorpe, a defender of Yorke.*

She could have sworn she felt the sword shift in the rock. Just an inch. Her heart leapt, and she thought she would lift the sword clean out of the rock.

But when she opened her eyes the sword was still stuck fast.

'Never mind,' said Miss Regemont kindly, seeing her disappointment. 'You are not a butler, Miss Raventhorpe. The sayings and stories may refer only to us. And strictly speaking, I am not a butler myself, but the head of Hall.' She turned to Heddsworth. 'I think this is your task. You're our head butler.'

Heddsworth stared at the sword. 'I don't know,' he murmured.

'You can do it!' said Rose. 'You have to!'

'If it doesn't work, we'll have to take the whole rock with us,' said Bronson.

Rose took hold of her cameo necklace again, feeling the carved image of the cat under her fingertips. The cameo had been a cherished gift. It held her Infinity Key. It was also her link with the cat statues of Yorke. She hoped the cats, her fellow guardians, were paying attention at this moment.

Heddsworth dusted off his white gloves. He wrapped his hands carefully around the sword hilt. Braced himself. And lifted.

The rock creaked. Rust flakes fell from the sword. Heddsworth heaved with all his might.

There was an ear-splitting crack. An explosion of dust. The sword came free, glinting in the sun. It was as silver-bright as an Infinity Key.

Everyone cheered. They clapped Heddsworth on the back, and reverently dusted off the sword.

'Goodness,' murmured Heddsworth. 'My word.'

At that moment Rose noticed several sheep wandering about the stone circle. The bells around their necks clanged.

'Bells!' she said. 'The bells in the rhyme!'

Nobody heard her. Everyone was too busy admiring Sigandus.

'I need a cup of tea,' said Heddsworth. And he sat down heavily on the ground, still staring in awe at the blade.

*

Miss Regemont was thrilled with their find. 'What a fine blade it will be, once it has been properly cleaned. A ceremonial blade of course, not like a proper rapier, but still a splendid piece of history. We have you to thank, Miss Wildcliffe. You must keep it safe until we can return to the Hall.'

'Gladly,' said Miss Wildcliffe. 'Oh, if Brannion could have seen this!'

Rose took a turn at holding the heavy sword. She preferred her own rapier, she decided. But it was still a very beautiful weapon.

They returned happily to Withering Downs. Miss Wildcliffe's good mood lasted until she checked her pantry. There was very little left in the way of food.

'I shall have to go into the city in the wagon and buy some more,' she said. 'I have credit with some of the shopkeepers.'

'I'm very sorry, Miss Wildcliffe,' said Miss Regemont. 'We do hope to return home as soon as possible.'

'You helped me to find the sword Brannion sought half his life,' said Miss Wildcliffe. 'I am grateful for that. You may all stay as long as you like.'

'We'll come with you into the city,' said Rose. 'The butlers can't risk it, but Orpheus can come with me. Inaaya can stay here, she's having a wonderful time.'

'I know,' said Orpheus ruefully. 'She's adopted those triplet lambs. Tonight she's going to sleep in the shed with them.'

Miss Wildcliffe hummed as she drove the wagon. 'I wish I'd brought Wolf with me,' she told the children. 'But he's getting plenty of attention back at home.'

'It's probably safer for him there,' said Rose. She and Orpheus sat in the back of the wagon, on top of the hay, basking in the sunshine. It was fun to be in a donkey-drawn wagon – a lord's daughter had few chances to do something like that.

But as they rolled down Ravensgate they heard a shout, and a swarm of Wakemen surrounded the carriage. Miss Wildcliffe tried to calm the frightened donkey, while Rose and Orpheus climbed on to the seat to help her.

'How dare you?' Rose snapped at the Wakemen.

Then Bathory appeared out of the group. 'This is an arrest,' he told her, brandishing his sword. 'Miss Jane Wildcliffe, otherwise known as the Moorland Witch, is suspected of raising the legendary Barghest, causing the death of an innocent woman and nearly killing the mayor. She's coming with us.'

The scene erupted into chaos. Miss Wildcliffe was dragged from the wagon, fighting with all her might. Onlookers watched, some cheered while others frowned. Rose and Orpheus did their best to protect Miss Wildcliffe, but they had no chance against so many Wakemen.

'This isn't justice!' Rose shouted. 'You'll be disbanded and disgraced, I swear!'

Then she was set on her feet, her hair a tangled

mess and her coat torn. Orpheus was forced to stand next to her, held by three men. Bathory grinned at Rose. 'Now, my Ladyship, your papa will be glad to know we rescued you from the wicked witch.' He lifted an eyebrow. 'Why are you with her? Where are your butler friends? Has the witch been plotting against us?'

'You can't blame Miss Wildcliffe for the attacks,' she retorted. 'You have no evidence whatsoever.'

'We'll see, won't we, my dear? Take the witch to the Hall. Better let the brats go,' he ordered his friends. 'They're no use to us. They can ride home with the donkey.'

'Wait!' cried Rose. She scrambled after Bathory. 'You can't take the law into your own hands like this! Not even the mayor would allow it.'

'The mayor will understand,' said Bathory. People will be grateful to us for locking the witch up. If she doesn't get sentenced to prison, a mental asylum should do nicely.'

'We'll pay her bail!' shouted Orpheus.

'We can't allow that,' sniffed Bathory piously. 'We can't allow a witch to escape.'

Rose gulped. She could only think of one way to save Miss Wildcliffe.

'Wait,' she cried. 'An exchange. We can offer something better than money. The sword of Sigandus.'

Orpheus made a shocked noise. 'Don't, Rose!' he hissed against her ear. 'You can't! It's a famous relic, it's powerful – and they won't honour a bargain.'

'I know, but we can't let this happen!'

Bathory pushed Orpheus away from Rose. 'Sigandus?' he exclaimed. 'You really have it? Or are you lying?'

'We do, and we can get it for you,' said Rose. 'We've found it.'

The Wakeman smirked. 'Maybe we should have a little talk. Come along then, into our nice new Hall. We'll even tie up your wagon outside. Can't say we don't treat you well.'

He let them through the Hall's door, with a

group of Wakemen as their escort. They followed him through the Hall's beautiful rooms, passing the kitchen on the way. Food was scattered everywhere, dirty dishes towering on the sink. Rose wrinkled her nose. The butlers would be horrified.

They walked through the sword display room. It was usually full of swords from all over the world: scimitars, claymores, jewelled rapiers, sabres, branched swords and samurai blades. The display cases had been broken open and the swords removed.

Orpheus pointed to a sideboard. 'Gone!' he whispered. 'The silver candlesticks, the trays, the tea service, the cutlery – what have they done with it?'

'Sold it, most likely,' whispered Rose.

They reached the library. A fire was burning in the hearth. Bathory and Glyde sat down in comfortable armchairs, and picked up glasses of wine. The children were left standing with their guards. Hunting trophies and garish portraits hung on the walls, having replaced the butlers' collections of rare porcelain and paintings. There were tiger-skin rugs, stag heads, elephant feet and rifles. Bathory was using a copy of *Pride and Prejudice* to keep the fire burning. Rose whispered Gaelic and Arabic swearwords under her breath.

Miss Wildcliffe was brought in, struggling against a burly Wakeman who had to hold a hand over her mouth to keep her quiet. She made muffled sounds of outrage.

'Here she is,' said Bathory. 'Safe and sound! Not a scratch on her. Now, what is this about the sword of Sigandus? Do you actually have it? You'd better not be spinning a tale. She'll pay for it.' He jerked his head at Miss Wildcliffe.

'We do.' Rose gave him her angriest look. 'But before we give it to you, you must agree to release Miss Wildcliffe, allow the butlers to return, and tell the people of Yorke that the Barghest isn't real!'

'Oh, but the Barghest *is* real,' said Bathory, inspecting his fingernails. 'The city needs us to protect the people from this dreadful curse. The police have failed to stop the crimes, so we have taken them off the case.'

'How convenient for you,' said Rose coldly. 'And the mayor being attacked was convenient too.'

Glyde scowled at her. 'What are you saying? We didn't do any harm to the mayor.'

'The attack on the mayor has allowed you to take over the city. So yes, it is very convenient for you that the mayor is in hospital!'

To Rose's annoyance, Bathory snickered. 'This is all very entertaining, but we didn't attack the mayor. If he recovers I'm sure he will let us keep this Hall when he learns how hard we've worked to protect this little city of his.'

'I doubt he was hurt badly enough to believe that,' muttered Orpheus.

Rose glared at the Wakeman. 'So if you didn't harm him, who – or what – did?'

Bathory shrugged. 'That dog of Miss Wildcliffe's did the deed if you ask me, and she deserves punishment for it. That beast's a killer if I ever saw one. It nearly attacked Glyde in the street. The next time you bring it into the city I'll string it up by the neck and make an example of it.'

Miss Wildcliffe struggled again, managing to kick her captor in the leg.

'You're the crazy ones, not Miss Wildcliffe,' said Orpheus. He was trembling with fury.

'Maybe you didn't kill Moll the Pocket, Bathory,' said Rose. 'But you could have copied that crime to get the mayor out of the way.'

The Wakemen stared at her. Either they were good actors or they seemed genuinely surprised. 'Very funny,' said Bathory at last. 'It worked out well for us, yes. Frankly, we're grateful to whoever put the mayor out of action. But it wasn't us!'

Rose knew better than to accept their words as truth. Yet, if the Wakemen were the culprits, she still lacked evidence.

'Enough of this,' said Bathory. 'It's the sword I want. Do you have it?'

Rose stepped forward.

'We have,' she said. 'Not here, but somewhere safe. If you let Miss Wildcliffe go, and lift the ban from the butlers of Yorke, you may have it.'

Miss Wildcliffe made a horrified noise. Orpheus groaned. Bathory leaned forwards intently. 'I knew it must be in Yorke,' he said. 'If you have it, prove it.'

Rose shook her head. 'Not until you set Miss Wildcliffe at liberty, and revoke that ban.'

The Wakeman sighed. 'I'm out of patience with this. I want the sword now. If you want your witch to go free, you'd better produce it.' He took out a pistol. 'Tell me where it is now.'

Rose's heart sank. *I should have seen this coming*, she thought.

There was a polite throat-clearing from the doorway and they all jumped as Heddsworth stepped into the room. His pistol was trained on Bathory. 'Please lower that gun, Bathory. I would rather talk than do something regrettable.'

'Dear me, we have a hero in the making here!'

sneered Bathory. 'Are the rest of your friends here? Is this how you mean to get your Hall back? You're still outnumbered, butler.'

'Not today,' said Heddsworth. 'Perhaps you could let the children and the lady leave.'

'How did you get in?' Bathory demanded. 'Through a back window?'

'The front door,' said Heddsworth. 'I was forced to knock your guard on the head. He will probably still be unconscious.' He glanced at Rose. 'I apologise for following you all, but I was rather fearful that Miss Wildcliffe might run into trouble. I didn't expect it to be quite this severe.' Rose felt a wave of shame and relief.

Then the sound of running feet was heard on the staircase. The clatter of weapons. More Wakemen were coming to stop the intruder.

'Quickly!' said Heddsworth.

They ran. They ran for the front door, as if by mutual consent. 'Stop them!' Bathory shouted.

Miss Wildcliffe's shawl tore as she bolted down

the passageway, shielding Rose and Orpheus. Rose heard a pistol shot, and felt a cold rush of terror.

Then they were outside on the doorstep of the Hall, rushing down the street into the sunshine. They ran past the wagon, knocking into startled people, gasping for breath. Rose ducked into a skitterway and her friends followed. Rose, sneaking a look around the corner, saw two cloaked Wakemen in the distance slow down. Having lost sight of their quarry, they shrugged at each other, and turned back towards the Hall.

Rose and her friends had made it. Miss Wildcliffe had been rescued.

'Is anyone hurt?' Rose demanded. 'Miss Wildcliffe? Orpheus?'

She turned to see Miss Wildcliffe and Orpheus catch Heddsworth, who was swaying on his feet. Blood darkened his white shirtfront and trickled down to the cobblestones of Ravensgate.

Chapter 12

A Moment on the Wall

Rose was dreaming of the moors. Heddsworth sat next to her on a low wall – a low, winding, drystone wall. It was sunny and peaceful.

'What kind of wall is this?' she asked.

'This,' said Heddsworth, 'is a drystone wall. They were built to keep sheep from wandering. Works of art, these walls.' He looked around the sunny moor. 'Do you know, Miss Raventhorpe, that some of the oldest walls of this kind were used to keep out wolves?'

Rose shivered. She felt surprisingly cold despite the sun.

Heddsworth held out some small stones. 'Hearting-stones,' he said. 'That is the name of the filling stones in these walls. They keep the bigger stones secure. The longer stones are called the through-stones.'

'I like those names,' said Rose.

'And if you move some of the stones down by the ground,' he pointed to the base of the wall, 'you'll see there is a smoot-hole, a little passageway for smaller animals. Bigger ones are called creep-holes, to let the sheep through where necessary.' He smiled. 'Every good wall has a means of getting through.'

A breeze blew Rose's hair as she climbed down to look at the neat space in the wall. How clever, she thought.

Then, without warning, Heddsworth climbed down the wall on the other side from Rose. He began to walk across the moor.

'Where are you going?' Rose asked, startled.

'Oh, we all cross this wall some time,' he called back.

'But you can't go yet,' Rose protested. She tried to climb up the wall again, but it suddenly seemed too high, too smooth for footholds. Feeling panicked, Rose began to move some of the wall stones. 'You can come back this way.'

A bird flew overhead, singing sweetly. With increasing urgency Rose tugged at the stones. She didn't want to destroy the beautiful wall, but she had to bring Heddsworth back. She tried to dismantle the wall. Heddsworth kept walking. He was nearly out of sight.

Then Rose heard snarling. She turned, hairs rising on the nape of her neck.

Fierce red eyes that glowed like fire. A menacing body too large for a mortal dog.

The Barghest stalked forward, its red eyes fixed on Heddsworth.

Rose shook all over. 'Don't you touch him,' she

ordered. Her hands found stones. She threw them. It yelped, and snarled again. 'Don't you dare!'

The snarls were deafening now. The Barghest crouched, ready to leap over the wall.

And Rose woke with a panicked heart, in the spare room at Withering Downs.

The butlers at Withering Downs struggled to keep up their spirits. Miss Regemont tried to assure everyone that Heddsworth would survive. The hospital staff were doing their best. But none of it really helped Rose.

She had taken a stupid risk, bargaining with Bathory, and now Heddsworth could be dying. Orpheus tried to speak some words of comfort, but she knew he was feeling bad enough himself.

Miss Regemont told Rose it would be difficult to have Bathory arrested while the mayor was still in hospital. Heddsworth had been armed, and technically trespassing since the butlers had been expelled from the Hall. Some judges might see

Bathory's action as justified. 'Heddsworth could end up in more trouble than he needs at present,' Miss Regemont said bitterly.

Miss Wildcliffe said very little. She set off for the moors every morning with Wolf, and came back only at dusk. One morning Rose got up at dawn herself, and stole downstairs. She went out into the sunlit moors. It was pleasant to be alone with the wind and the heather. She followed a sheep track and found Miss Wildcliffe and her dog sitting by a small waterfall. Tea-brown water poured over the rocks. Rose heard croaking frogs and the rustling wind, bird calls and the distant moos of cattle. The air was deliciously cold and pure, the new grass soft as moss.

Miss Wildcliffe saw Rose, and patted the grass beside her.

'I'm surprised you are still here, Miss Raventhorpe. Don't you want to go home?'

'No,' said Rose. 'Not without Heddsworth.' She paused. 'I can see why you like it here. It's beautiful.'

Miss Wildcliffe sighed. 'Most people don't appreciate it. They only want their fine houses and grand carpets and silly affectations.'

'I think you're wrong,' said Rose. 'A lot would want to live like you. With your hawk and your dog.'

'They'd be lonely,' growled Miss Wildcliffe.

Rose pondered that. 'Sometimes. It's nice to have human company, isn't it? And buildings can be beautiful too. Like the cathedral.'

Miss Wildcliffe shrugged. 'I prefer the simple and honest to the ornate.'

'I like simple and honest too,' Rose protested. 'But the cathedral is one of man's great works. A song in stone. Like the Book of Kells.'

'I couldn't live in a walled city,' said Miss Wildcliffe. 'I would feel imprisoned.'

'Not everyone does.'

'Yes,' said Miss Wildcliffe. 'You are proof of that.' She paused. 'I'm sorry about Heddsworth,' she added abruptly. 'I should never have gone into the city knowing the Wakemen were running the place. I shouldn't have allowed you to come with me.'

'It's not your fault,' said Rose miserably. 'It's mine. I shouldn't have offered Bathory the sword.'

'You're not the one who shot Heddsworth,' said Miss Wildcliffe. 'It's the Wakemen who should be sorry. Have you heard any news of the Lord Mayor's state of health?'

'The newspapers say he's still not well,' said Rose. 'Do you still have Sigandus? I wish we'd never set eyes on it now.'

'Yes, it's safe and sound in my room. At least the Wakemen didn't get it.' Miss Wildcliffe sighed. 'I'm touched that you tried to bargain it for me, Miss Raventhorpe, but they would never have honoured a bargain. Bathory would have taken the sword and sent me off to an asylum or a prison.'

'I know. I'm sorry,' said Rose.

'That's all right.' Miss Wildcliffe gazed across the moors, and started. 'Look!' she exclaimed, smiling. 'More butlers!'

Rose followed her gaze. A steady stream of butlers was walking down the road to Withering Downs. Some carried sturdy overnight bags, while others bore suitcases or trunks. Rose and Miss Wildcliffe hurried after them towards the house. Miss Regemont and the other butlers spilled outdoors to greet the visitors.

'Towzel!' exclaimed Miss Regemont. 'You received my letter?'

A smiling red-headed butler beamed at Miss Regemont. 'At your service, madam! I bring you the butlers of Brighton and Cornwall.'

'What a journey!' said one, dusting off his coat. 'All the way to the wilds of the North!'

'How splendid that you could come to our aid,' said Miss Regemont warmly.

'We did have difficulties in arranging to take time off, but we came as soon as we could,' said Towzel. 'We shall see off those rogues! Stealing the Hall from you! Whatever next?'

'They shot Heddsworth too,' said Miss

Regemont. She winced at their exclamations of dismay. 'But it will take more than a bullet to end our Heddsworth.'

'I'm longing to see the Stairs Below again,' said Towzel. 'And the, what are they called again? Sneak-aways?'

'Skitterways,' said Charlie Malone.

'In Brighton we have catscreeps and twittens,' said another butler. 'Our own little alleys. You should all visit.'

'Perhaps after we have sorted out the current crisis,' said Miss Regemont.

'Grand,' said Towzel. He peered back down the road. 'More are coming. From other countries. They made remarkably good time, considering they had to take trains and ships after Miss Regemont sent out the word.'

'Just where are we going to put everyone?' Miss Wildcliffe worried. 'In tents? How many more mouths to feed? I didn't get any more supplies from Yorke.'

The butlers exchanged awkward looks. 'We have brought some refreshments with us,' offered Towzel. 'They should keep us going for a day or two.'

'We can camp out of doors on this charming estate,' said another butler. He turned hopefully to Miss Wildcliffe. 'What about other local houses? Farming concerns? Would they like to board a few of us? We shall do our best to repay them.'

'I suppose Gowkins might help,' said Miss Wildcliffe. 'I shall walk to his farm and inquire.' She stalked off.

'Right,' said Bronson, squaring her shoulders. 'It is time for a council of war.'

The council of war took place in the chicken coop.

Several butlers were in the middle of cleaning the house, and refused to allow anyone to step on the floor. The chicken coop had been meticulously tidied, and the chickens were out in the garden. It was just big enough for everyone to sit inside. Dozens of tents had been set up all around Withering Downs, with Miss Wildcliffe's permission, to accommodate the new arrivals.

The Cornish butlers had brought pasties and scones, and challenged Bronson to a duel over the correct order of scone toppings. 'Oh dear,' murmured Charlie Malone. 'The "jam or cream first" debate. It always turns violent.'

Miss Regemont settled herself with as much ceremony as if she was in her office at the Hall. 'Mr Malone, are you ready for note-taking?'

'Certainly madam,' said Charlie, writing pad at the ready.

'Very well. Let the council begin. Our Hall has been seized by ruffians, and we need to recover it without grievous injury or loss of life, if it can be helped. Investigation of the Stairs Below shows the Wakemen have blocked off the entrance to the Hall – perhaps unwittingly, with rubble from the attack. We do not know if they realise what the Stairs Below is. However, we still have our Infinity

Keys and can clear away the rubble if we choose to attack that way.'

'Hear, hear!' said Towzel. 'A siege at dawn! With rapiers and pistols!'

'We must plan this carefully,' warned Miss Regemont. 'We are butlers, not blundering idiots.'

'I think dawn is a good time,' Charlie ventured. 'From what we've heard of the Wakemen, they are not the best sentries.' He looked at Rose. 'Isn't that so? When you went to the Hall, how many men were present?'

'About twenty,' she offered. 'I'm not certain. But I don't think they know how we use the Stairs Below. They didn't mention it.'

'Helpful,' said Miss Regemont, making a note. 'They may not expect an attack from that quarter. Even if they do, I think we should chance it. Anything else?'

Rose forced herself to think. 'They're untidy and they've drunk a lot of your wine.'

'Scoundrels,' muttered Miss Regemont. 'Even the port and the claret?'

'Er, probably.'

'So you think they may be drunk on duty?'

'Entirely possible,' said Rose.

'Also helpful. What about weapons?'

'They've taken most of the swords,' said Orpheus. 'But I doubt they've kept them. Sold them, more likely.'

Miss Regemont's lips compressed. 'Very well. I suggest flank attacks from all quarters at once. One attack from the roof – I have sent word to the sweeps of the Raven Society to assist us there – and an attack via the Stairs Below.'

'We should draw them out,' agreed Bronson. 'Spread out their forces, divide them.'

'Excellent!' said Orpheus. 'We're in.'

'"We"?' said Miss Regemont. 'I hardly think you are going to take part in an attack, either you or Miss Raventhorpe. This kind of attack is known as a Vainglory.'

'A what?' said Orpheus.

'A Vainglory is an attack that usually fails, but is necessary to draw out the enemy,' Miss Regemont explained. 'We shall try to draw them out of the Hall. As Bronson said, spread their forces.'

'Oh,' said Orpheus. 'Like firing a cannon from a ship when you're out of range?'

'Something like that,' said Miss Regemont. 'We now have the numbers to make up a surprise attack.'

'We are to attack tomorrow, yes?' asked a French butler. 'We are prepared, madame.'

'I look forward to it, ma'am,' said an American, loading his pistol.

'I'm a nervous wee wreck,' said a Scottish butler, hefting his claymore over one powerful shoulder. 'No offence, madam, but are we no' goin' to leave this chicken coop?'

'Ah,' said Miss Regemont. 'Yes.' She dusted a stray feather from her skirt. 'Of course. Come along, everyone. We need some rest before our dawn attack.'

Rose and Orpheus took the Raventhorpe carriage home to Yorke. With Lady Constance still in London, Rose thought it safe to invite Orpheus to stay in a guest room. They took turns holding the sword of Sigandus. The butlers had polished it, cleaned off rust and sharpened it.

'So, we're not to take part in this siege,' said Orpheus sadly. 'I suppose we can't blame them after what happened last time in the Hall.'

'I know,' said Rose. 'But there is something we *can* do. We can visit Heddsworth in hospital.'

'Miss Regemont doesn't want him upset,' Orpheus pointed out. 'And he might not be up to visitors.'

'We won't upset him,' said Rose. 'I want to take him the sword of Sigandus.'

'Why?' asked Orpheus. 'He needs doctors, not a sword.' He stared at Rose. 'Don't tell me you've started to believe in the Barghest? Do you think that Heddsworth needs it for protection?'

Rose shifted uncomfortably. 'I don't know.' She took a deep breath and, feeling rather silly, told Orpheus about her dream, with Heddsworth walking away across the moor pursued by the ghostly hound. 'I remembered that Brannion thought the sword would save him when he was at death's door,' she explained. 'And I just can't help wondering whether it might do Heddsworth some good.'

Orpheus grinned. 'I never thought I'd see the day that you believed in a ghost hound,' he said. 'But it won't do him any harm. 'Shall we take him some food as well?'

'Tea,' suggested Rose. 'And a cucumber sandwich.'

'If anything would revive Heddsworth from the brink, it's that,' said Orpheus.

They directed Jeremiah to take them to a tea shop, where the staff happily packed the gifts in a box. Then they walked to the hospital.

Heddsworth lay asleep in a bed, terribly pale.

'He oughtn't to be disturbed, miss,' said a nurse in warning.

'We won't bother him,' whispered Rose. Tears threatened under her eyelids.

She and Orpheus sat by the bed. The nurse fussed around, then left to give them some privacy.

'We've brought the sword, Heddsworth,' whispered Rose. 'If you are on the wall, you will have this to fight with. Don't let the Barghest take you.' She poured tea from a flask into the porcelain cup. She looked covertly around the ward, and dropped her voice. 'They're planning to besiege the Hall tomorrow.'

'The sweeps are going to help,' added Orpheus.

'And,' said Rose, 'I thought perhaps Orpheus and I could patrol the city walls and watch the siege from there. We want to be there to help the butlers if they need it.'

'We'll try to keep out of trouble,' Orpheus clarified.

'And you mustn't worry either,' said Rose.

'There are plenty of butlers at Withering Downs now, and they will help to take the Hall back. We want you back at home. Mrs Standish would cook wonderful food for you. You can rest in proper comfort there.'

'I can help,' promised Orpheus. 'I can set the table, and iron newspapers and everything.'

Heddsworth did not stir. Rose struggled to keep her emotions under control. She thought of her dream. That wall. The monstrous dog coming for Heddsworth.

She lifted the sword of Sigandus and placed it gently beside him, on top of the coverlet.

'Look after this for us,' she whispered. 'We'll tell the nurses it is not to be disturbed. We're going to take back the Hall. And we're going to find out who – or what – is attacking people,' she added. 'We're going to stop it, Heddsworth. It's not going to hurt anyone else.'

But before the day ended, she would discover she was wrong.

Chapter 13

Let Slip the Butlers of War

Rose was preparing for bed that night when she heard a shriek downstairs.

She grabbed a lighted candle and hurried down in her nightgown. Orpheus came running from his room. Agnes the maid was at the door. A shocked-looking Lorimer stood there.

'I'm so sorry to bother you all,' he stammered. 'But I wasn't sure where else to go – I don't trust the Wakemen, but the police have been taken off the case.' He took a deep breath. 'There has been another attack.'

'We can't go out of doors no more!' cried Agnes. 'The beast of Yorke is stalkin' the city.'

Rose patted Agnes soothingly on the arm, but her own nerves were all on end.

'It attacked Sylvia Prentiss,' said Lorimer. 'In the skitterway by the shop. Again, in Mad Meg Lane.'

'Sylvia? Your shop assistant?' cried Rose. 'Is she – alive?'

'Yes, miss,' said Lorimer miserably. 'She took a blow to the head, and has some scratches. But she's alive.'

'Thank heavens for that,' said Rose. 'We must go to the skitterway at once.'

'Oh, miss, not at this time of night!' wailed Agnes. 'Not with the Barghest about! Not with Mr Heddsworth ill!'

'We'll be with Lorimer, and we'll take our

rapiers,' said Orpheus. 'The Barghest won't get us, Agnes.'

'Lord, but it would give me a turn to see that beast,' said Agnes. 'I'd die of fright, I would.'

'Were you nearby when it happened, Lorimer? Who raised the alarm?' Rose wanted to know.

'I was wrapping chocolates in our workshop, not an hour past,' said Lorimer. 'I had no idea that Miss Prentiss was in the skitterway until I heard her cry out. Then I rushed out and found her unconscious on the ground, with some nasty scratches to her arm. I carried her into the shop at once, and raised the alarm. Dr Jankers came to attend her.'

'Will she be all right?'

'I hope so, miss. The doctor is very angry about this, naturally.' Lorimer shivered. 'The Barghest has never been so vicious in all the city's history.'

'Let me get dressed and we'll go back with you,' Rose told Lorimer. She hurried to put on some warm clothes and fetch her rapier. Then she ran downstairs and joined Lorimer and Orpheus.

Lorimer had taken a hansom cab to Lambsgate, and they returned in it to the Shudders. The lamps had been lit at the Chocolate Emporium. Lorimer unlocked the front door and led them in. The delicious smells of chocolate and sweets seemed wildly at odds with the circumstances.

Sylvia had been made comfortable on the floor with a pile of cushions. She looked pale and her eyes were closed. Dr Jankers was attending to the ugly scratches on her arm.

'How is she?' Rose crouched to see the patient.

'Coming round,' said Dr Jankers. 'I can't believe she went out into the skitterway on her own! Thought she had more sense.'

'I believe she heard a noise, and went outside to investigate. She took a saucepan out with her, probably as a weapon,' said Lorimer. 'It was near her hand when I found her.'

'That sounds like something she would do,' said Jankers. 'Sylvia? Can you hear me?'

Sylvia stirred, and muttered something. It sounded like, 'Eyes'.

'Sylvia?' said Rose softly. 'Do you remember what happened to you?'

'Head – hurts,' said Sylvia.

'Yes. Someone hit you.'

'Heard noise,' Sylvia muttered. 'Looked outside. Red flames. Like eyes.'

Rose looked at Orpheus. Lorimer whimpered.

'Wanted to catch him,' Sylvia went on. 'Murderer. Went after him.'

'The murderer?' Rose caught her breath. So Sylvia wasn't the culprit. She felt a sickening lurch of guilt that she had considered Sylvia as a suspect. It took extreme bravery to run out into that skitterway and confront a potential killer, armed with nothing but a saucepan.

'What did you see, Sylvia? Do you know who it might have been?'

'Dark,' said Sylvia. She frowned painfully. 'Went after the eyes. Then something hit me.'

'You were very courageous,' said Rose.

'And foolhardy,' said Dr Jankers, but he patted Sylvia's shoulder. 'Silly thing to do. City's full of thieves and ruffians. My own Medical School was broken into last week. Lost some bottles of chemicals and powders.'

Rose sat back on the floor. 'Maybe the villain has an accomplice,' she said, thinking aloud. 'The victims see the eyes in the skitterway, but someone hits them from behind.'

'Maybe,' said Orpheus. 'That would be the sort of the thing the Wakemen would do.'

'Whoever did it, they've got the city scared,' said Dr Jankers gruffly. 'And this won't help.'

Sylvia struggled up, rubbing at her head. She looked at Rose pleadingly. 'Can I talk to you alone?'

'Of course,' said Rose, surprised. The others were startled, but after an awkward pause they all left the room.

'What is it?' asked Rose.

'I know who was behind the ploy with the dead dog in the alley,' whispered Sylvia. 'It was Mr Rawlings.'

'*What*?'

'I overheard him talking to the Wakemen in Mad Meg Lane,' Sylvia continued. 'He said the mayor was worried by the attack on the pickpocket. Thought that people were bound to panic and he would have disorder on his hands. He said the mayor wanted the Wakemen to fake the death of the Barghest, using a stray dog. I didn't tell anyone. I thought it was a good idea. That it would stop the panic.' She paused to rub her head again. 'Then—'

'The mayor was attacked,' finished Rose. She tried to digest all this new information. 'And now you,' said Rose softly. 'Oh, Sylvia, you care far too much about the shop! Your uncle wouldn't want you killed!'

'I want the shop to succeed because I want to study at the Medical School,' said Sylvia, to Rose's utter astonishment. 'Uncle wouldn't let me. He said I had to prove myself at the shop – to be competent and skilful – before he'd consider it.'

'So that's why you cared so much,' breathed Rose. 'Now I understand!'

'Rose – I didn't believe in the Barghest before, but now I don't know what to think,' whispered Sylvia. 'I thought it was a normal dog. But I saw the red eyes, Rose! I didn't imagine them!'

Rose felt troubled. 'We need to find out who is doing this. When the mayor is up and about we can ask him about his attacker. But I don't believe there's a spectral dog. A real person struck you down, and I mean to find out why.'

When she left the shop and went out into the skitterway Rose saw people with lanterns peering down, whispering in scared voices.

'The devil dog has struck again!'

'Struck a girl stone dead, just by lookin' at her!'

'That witch from the moor – she's to blame.

I've heard she escaped the Wakemen. They need to lock her up.'

Sergeant Snodgrass appeared, looking anxious and out of temper. 'Not you two again!' he exclaimed, at the sight of Rose and Orpheus.

'Have you found anything?' called Rose.

'Now look, this is police business! Not a place for children. You must go home,' he addressed the fearful crowd. 'If there's still a wild dog out there, you don't want it after you. Clear the skitterway!' he bellowed, and there was a scuffling of feet.

'Oh, bother it,' said Rose. 'This is horrible. Sylvia could have been killed.' She set her chin. 'We're going to take part in that siege tonight, Orpheus. We are going to help the butlers get the Hall back. We need them here to defend the city. We are going to get rid of those Wakemen and then we will catch that murderer.'

'And I thought I'd have to talk you into it,' said Orpheus, tugging at her elbow. 'Well, what a relief. I didn't want to do all the heroics by myself.'

Rose paused. Something had caught her eye in the skitterway – a pine cone. She bent and picked it up. You found all sorts of rubbish in skitterways, but this struck her as odd. Why would someone drop a pine cone? Was it an old Christmas ornament?

'Hurry, Rose!' hissed Orpheus, and she dropped the pine cone in her pocket.

Rose and Orpheus were up in the pale light of dawn, stumbling in their efforts to dress quickly. They cleaned their rapiers and snatched some breakfast.

'We'll leave by the window in the butler's pantry,' Rose whispered. 'And go to the walls, as close to the Hall as we can.'

'Sounds like a good plan.' Orpheus straightened his tricorn hat.

They scurried down the dark streets. The city seemed peaceful and normal, rustling with the beginnings of the day: pedlars and wagons, clerks and laundresses, neighing horses, street sweepers.

Rose and Orpheus climbed the stairs to the Yorke wall and studied the view of the city. They were not far from Ravensgate and Silvercrest Hall.

Just then a sound made them turn, and Rose's heart leapt into her mouth. Two Wakemen she didn't recognise were coming towards them on the wall.

Rose and Orpheus pelted down the wall-top. This section was so narrow they had to run in single file. Rose hoped that this would slow the Wakemen down too.

Then another person loomed in front of her. Rose skidded to a halt. Bronson grinned at them. 'I knew you two would try something.'

One of the Wakemen had caught up to them. 'This wall is off-limits to everyone but the Wakemen!' he shouted. He caught sight of Bronson's rapier. 'Wait a minute. Aren't you the female butler? The upstart housekeeper?'

Bronson made a quick movement and a rapier-point nestled at his throat.

'I am *not* a housekeeper,' said Bronson. 'I am a butler, just as you are a piece of—'

'Watch out!' Two more Wakemen were approaching from their other side. Rose drew her own rapier. Orpheus swore under his breath. They were surrounded.

'I had no idea they all got up this early,' complained Bronson. 'Backs to me, you two.'

Rose and Orpheus obeyed. Rose watched the Wakemen nervously. Bronson was a brilliant swordswoman, but could she hold off four grown men?

'Now,' said Bronson to the nearest Wakemen, 'I'm sure you don't want your friend killed on this nice clean wall, so please let us through like gentlemen.'

The Wakemen hesitated.

'Let ' em go!' croaked the Wakeman with the sword at his throat.

Muttering, the others moved away.

'That's right. Further back,' said Bronson. 'Past the steps.'

They obeyed.

'That's better,' said Bronson. She lowered her voice so that only Orpheus and Rose could hear. 'Go Watchful's way. Try to find a soft landing.'

The three of them leapt over the side of the wall.

It was only an eight-foot drop on to grass. Still, it jarred Rose's whole body, and she wished she was a cat like Watchful.

'Oww,' said Orpheus. 'Lucky I didn't land on my rapier.'

Rose hauled him to his feet. The angry Wakemen were climbing down the wall in pursuit, shouting for their friends. A dozen more appeared, running across the wall top. 'Run!' cried Bronson. They did, following hard on her heels.

'Miss Raventhorpe, your Infinity Key!' yelled Bronson.

Rose flicked open her cameo to extract the key. They sprinted towards the nearest skitterway. Bronson was more familiar with this area than

Rose, and swiftly located a door to the Stairs Below.

Bronson stood guard while Rose inserted the key, her hands trembling. She got the door open. Orpheus pushed her down the steps. Rose heard the clash of swords. Then Bronson burst through the doorway.

They slammed the door behind them, and Rose locked it. They heard Bronson strike a match. She reached for a lantern hanging on the wall. Light flared, and they saw each other's faces. Bronson's was exhilarated.

'Anyone hurt?'

'No,' chorused Rose and Orpheus. Anything short of broken bones and deep gashes could wait.

'Well, I hope that lured some of them away from the Hall,' said Bronson. She inspected her rapier in the dim light, and glanced at the children. 'Shall we see how they are doing?'

They advanced through the darkness, trying to

cover their lantern so it gave just enough light to walk by. Rose judged they were close to Silvercrest Hall when she heard faint shouts and the clash of rapiers.

Bronson gave the others a warning glance. Then she stepped forward, light-footed as a cat.

They could hear someone rushing towards them in the dark passageway. The lantern tilted dangerously. 'Who goes there?' the person cried. It was Charlie Malone.

'We do,' said Bronson. 'Have you broken through to the Hall yet?'

'We will,' said Charlie confidently. 'We have half a dozen butlers on the attack from this side, and the sweeps are attacking the roof.' He saw the children. 'Oh. You two, hang back, please.'

Rose nodded. She didn't fancy trying to fight someone in the pitch darkness of the Stairs Below.

More footsteps sounded behind them. Then came what Rose thought of as the International

Butlers' Brigade. A group of men of all ages, all in their hats and tailcoats and gloves, carrying rapiers and lanterns. They all looked happy at the prospect of a fight. Towzel was in the lead. 'On to the breach!' he said happily. 'Let's give them what for!'

Chapter 14

To Catch a Hound

The butlers cleared a hole in the rubble that the Wakemen had used to block the door.

There was an immediate clash of swords – the Wakemen were clearly waiting for them – and then the sound of pistol shots. Orpheus pulled Rose down to the ground. 'Are they mad?' he whispered. 'Those shots could ricochet off the walls of the Stairs Below and kill them!'

'If they haven't hurt anyone already,' muttered Rose.

She heard terse questions from Bronson. The shots may have been only in warning, but anyone could get in the way of a stray bullet, especially in the confined space of the Stairs Below.

Charlie Malone came limping back to them.

'No one badly hurt,' he assured the children. 'But stay back. We'll have them running, never fear.'

They heard a shout from Bronson. 'Ha, they're in retreat! Up to the roof, everyone!'

Rose and her friends hurried down the tunnel. 'Careful – it might be a trick!' Charlie shouted. 'We don't want to be ambushed.'

The butlers climbed past the wreck of the door, its sign – *Et gladio et polies* – lying on the ground. Rose stopped to pick up the crest with the motto engraved upon it. It made a useful shield.

Then they were streaming into the ballroom of Silvercrest Hall. Bronson and Charlie stepped carefully into the room. The International Butlers' Brigade exclaimed in horror. 'The mirror is dusty!'

'They have scratched the floor!' 'That painting is crooked!' 'Have they no shame?' In minutes they were dusting, rolling up sleeves, washing and polishing.

Bronson and Charlie headed upstairs. Rose and Orpheus followed them from a distance. They climbed all the way up to the attic, where there was a specially installed door in the roof.

They could hear the chaos of the fighting outside. Charlie and Bronson climbed the steps up and on to the roof. Rose climbed up next, cursing her petticoats. She saw that the sweeps had disarmed most of the Wakemen, and were guarding them closely. Glyde, the only Wakeman still fighting, was up against Fawney, the leader of the Raven Society of Sweeps. The Wakeman lashed out with his rapier, catching Fawney on the leg. Fawney's pet raven wheeled and dived. Glyde swore, putting his hand to his scalp and bringing it away bloody. He drew a pistol.

Bronson stepped in. She sent the pistol flying

with a flick of her rapier and Charlie held his to Glyde's throat. He backed up against a chimneypot.

'Enough,' warned Bronson. 'All your friends have yielded. The Hall is ours.'

Glyde lowered his rapier. 'We were sick of the place, anyway.'

'Where's Bathory?' demanded Bronson. 'He's your leader – why isn't he up here with you?'

'He's probably injured,' said Glyde sullenly. 'Go downstairs and look if you're so keen.'

'Injured? Run away more like,' said Charlie Malone with contempt. 'I hope we catch that would-be murderer. The rest of you can go back to London. The mayor will know the truth about you soon enough.'

'I would love to duel Bathory for shooting Heddsworth,' muttered Bronson. 'But I will leave that privilege to Heddsworth himself, once he recovers.' She nodded to the sweeps. 'Thank you for your help, gentlemen. We are in your debt. Fawney, we must attend to that injury.'

'It ain't much,' said Fawney, as his raven came to perch on his shoulder.

Rose and Orpheus climbed down the ladder and stood guard with their rapiers. Disarmed, Glyde followed them into the attic, guarded by Bronson. Charlie stayed on the rooftop to help the injured sweeps. Then all the Wakemen were marched downstairs to be expelled from the Hall. Bathory was not among them, and Rose suspected he had fled rather than deal with a mob of vengeful butlers. She asked her friends if she had seen him.

'I did,' said Charlie Malone. 'He slunk out of the fray like the coward he is. I bet he's halfway to London by now. He won't want to deal with us, after what he did to Heddsworth.'

The defeated Wakemen, disarmed and surly, trudged out of the Hall. 'Stupid place anyway,' Rose heard one of them mutter. 'I'll be glad to see the back of it.'

Some of the victorious butlers were involved

in making tea and fresh shortbread biscuits. Rose followed Bronson to the front door.

Miss Regemont appeared. She looked less than immaculate, but she was radiantly happy to have her Hall back.

'Everything seems to have gone well,' she said. 'I wrote to the mayor yesterday, explaining what was going on. This morning I received a letter from him. He has finally recovered, and expressed great anger at what the Wakemen have done. We did well to recover the Hall.'

'Is he still in hospital?' Rose wanted to know. She urgently wanted to speak to him about his attack, to see if it matched with Sylvia's account. 'Can we speak to him?'

'He is at home now,' said Miss Regemont. 'And he wants us to help find the villain who attacked him.'

Lord Mayor Edward Chesney had returned to his home near the cathedral, Fortunatus House. He sat behind his desk, wearing fading bruises and his usual grim expression. Rawlings the butler hovered at his side like a large protective bear. Rose, Orpheus, Miss Regemont and Heddsworth all perched on uncomfortable chairs. Rose looked around the room and saw that the Wakemen must have made free with it. The office was untidier than usual, and some pictures and articles of silver were missing. Rawlings would have a lot of work to do.

'Before you ask, I've sent the Wakemen back to London,' the mayor told the assembled butlers. 'Those that are still around to take my orders, that is. I can assure you I did not authorise their taking over of your Hall. They wrote that order themselves. It seems they did not expect me to recover from my injuries. Young wretches!'

'It was impertinent of them, sir,' said Miss Regemont, with admirable restraint. 'I fear they took advantage of their positions.'

'Hmmph,' said the Lord Mayor. 'Should have

realised young men can go off the rails. Bathory and Glyde let responsibility go to their heads. Well, a man has to show encouragement to the younger generation.'

'Quite,' said Miss Regemont, with a glance at Rose and Orpheus.

'Had to make an apology to the police too,' the mayor went on. 'The Wakemen treated them shabbily, I've been told. I should have shown more trust in them. Only doing their best, after all.'

'Glad to hear it,' said Miss Regemont. 'Sergeant Snodgrass seems a fair sort of officer. Sir – do you have any memory of the night you were attacked?'

'I saw nothing useful,' said the mayor. 'More's the pity.'

'But why were you in the skitterway that night?' Rose demanded. 'Alone, on foot? Were you searching for the murderer?'

'No, I wasn't,' the mayor snapped. 'I was visiting acquaintances near the Shudders.'

'In the middle of the night?' said Rose sceptically.

She glanced at Rawlings, but he avoided meeting her eyes.

'It's really none of your business, miss,' huffed the mayor.

'I'm sorry, but we're trying to catch a murderer.'

'It was a private matter, and I did not in the least expect to be attacked by anyone!'

'Very well,' said Miss Regemont in a placating tone. 'I am glad you had no part in the Wakemen's treacherous behaviour, sir.'

'But the Wakemen might have been the attackers,' said Rose.

The mayor looked taken aback. 'What do you mean? You think they killed that pickpocket?'

'They might have killed her to start a panic, knowing that they would be brought in to find the beast,' Rose explained. 'And then attacked you to get you out of the way. Bathory wanted to run Yorke himself.'

'If that is the case,' muttered the mayor, 'we should not have let them go!'

'Well, we haven't any evidence yet that it was them,' Rose admitted. 'And they aren't the only suspects. I thought Rawlings might have been involved.'

'Rawlings? How on earth could you suspect him?' demanded the mayor, glancing at his butler.

'You ordered him to tell the Wakemen to plant a dead dog in Mad Meg Lane, and display it as the culprit,' said Rose.

Rawlings started.

'Who told you that?' spluttered the mayor.

'It doesn't matter,' said Rose. 'But is it true?'

Mayor Chesney's jaw tightened until it looked like a brick wall.

'It was a foolish ploy,' he said at last. 'I should have thought better of it.'

'It may have been a deception, sir,' said Rawlings uncomfortably. 'But you meant well.'

'Then you really were responsible? Why do such a thing?' persisted Rose.

The mayor swallowed visibly. 'I meant only to

stop the nonsensical rumours! I gave the people what they needed to see – a mortal dog, safely dead.'

'But it was trickery, sir!' cried Miss Regemont. 'And you became a victim yourself.'

'Fitting, I suppose,' the mayor admitted. 'But I have had enough of this crazed ghost-dog business! Now I know a flesh-and-blood person attacked me, I intend to catch the wretch.'

'How can you be so sure, sir?' Rose asked curiously.

'This morning I received an anonymous tip-off.' The mayor took a piece of paper from his pocket. The message read:

Dear Sir,

The so-named 'Barghest' will appear at midnight tonight in Mad Meg Lane. This is your chance to stop him. Take a gun. He intends murder.

A Well-Wisher

'It could be a hoax, sir,' warned Miss Regemont.

'I'm aware of that,' the mayor replied. 'But what if it tells the truth? That is why I want you and your friends as witnesses. I will go back to that skitterway, but this time I will be armed, and I will have you watching.'

'You want us to go with you?' said Charlie Malone. 'We would have to be covert – we don't want to scare him off . . .'

'Yes, we must tread carefully,' said the mayor. 'The killer isn't likely to attack a crowd. No, I want you to stay outside the skitterway, out of sight, until I have need of help.'

'Well,' said Miss Regemont. 'You are a man of courage, Sir Edward.' She consulted the others with silent looks. Everyone nodded their agreement: they wanted to do this. 'But you must take care, sir. No haring off after a suspect without us.'

'No,' said the mayor. 'And I don't want the

police interfering. They won't let me take a risk like this.' He looked at Rose and Orpheus. 'The children shouldn't be involved.'

'We will be responsible for the children, sir,' said Bronson. 'Their butler, Heddsworth, is still in hospital.' She could not resist adding, 'Bathory shot him.'

'Shot him?' The mayor's eyebrows lifted. Rawlings gasped.

'Is the man recovering?' asked the mayor.

'We hope he will pull through, sir,' said Miss Regemont.

The Lord Mayor sighed. 'Then I all the more regret hiring the Wakemen. I should have put my trust in you instead. I hope we can work together going forwards, madam.'

'That would be satisfactory, sir,' said Miss Regemont.

'Very good. Let us meet here, before midnight. Then we go hunting for the so-called Barghest.'

*

The butlers were delighted at the prospect of a midnight patrol.

'Just what a Guardian should do!' said Bronson, as they gathered in the fencing salon of the Hall.

'We shall follow at a discreet distance. Just Heddsworth, Bronson, Mr Malone and myself,' said Miss Regemont. '

'What about us?' said Rose. 'Me and Orpheus? You need us.'

'With a potential lunatic out there, wielding sharp implements?' Miss Regemont folded her arms. 'I hardly think so.'

'We're honorary Guardians!' said Orpheus hotly. 'This is our case too. We've been investigating this since the start. You can't send us to bed like a pair of infants.'

'I won't have you hurt!' said Miss Regemont. 'Heddsworth would never forgive me.'

'Nothing might happen at all,' said Orpheus, rather sulkily.

'Please,' said Rose. 'Please, can't we come with you? We want to help.'

'No, Miss Raventhorpe. It's too dangerous.'

'It's not really,' Rose argued. 'We'll be surrounded by armed butlers, and the mayor will be there.'

'You can't know what will happen.'

'We'll stay out of trouble, I promise. We'll do everything you tell us to.'

Miss Regemont sighed. Then she said, 'I must be mad, but very well. I suppose we will all be there to protect you.'

'Miss Regemont, you're a brick!' yelled Orpheus.

'Quietly now, Master Orpheus,' admonished Miss Regemont. 'A good butler never raises his voice.'

The door of the fencing salon opened, and Inaaya ran in. 'I want to come too!' she begged Orpheus. 'I want to see the big dog.'

'No, you don't,' said Orpheus. 'You need to stay here and look after the Hall with the other butlers.'

'I don't want to.'

'Now, young lady,' said Miss Regemont, with kindly finality. 'It's too dangerous. We are going to catch some villains. It is no place for you.'

'I can catch villains.'

'Inaaya!' Orpheus grabbed his sister as she ran for the rack of practice swords. 'No!'

'It's not fair,' Inaaya wailed. 'I never get to do anything exciting. You treat me like a baby!'

'I'm sorry, Inaaya,' said Rose.

'So are we,' said Charlie Malone. 'When we come back we shall tell you every gory detail.'

Inaaya sighed. 'You'd better,' she told Charlie crossly.

Orpheus hugged her and she went out with dragging steps.

'It's admirable she wants to help,' said Miss Regemont with a smile. 'Still. I think it will be a *very* long time before we give that child an Infinity Key.'

Chapter 15

Midnight in the Skitterway

At half past eleven, Rose, Orpheus and the butlers took the Stairs Below to Fortunatus House, where the Lord Mayor was waiting.

'I am prepared,' he informed the visitors, holding up his pistol.

Miss Regemont frowned. 'I hope you won't need to use it, sir. We will all be armed ourselves.'

'I've been made a fool of by this ruffian long

enough,' growled the mayor. 'The villain was mortal, and I'm going to prove it. I'll take him out with my own pistol.'

'Very well, sir.'

The mayor consulted his fob watch. 'Time to go to the skitterway. Remember, I shall enter it alone. You may wait at a distance. Discreetly, mind!'

'Of course, sir.'

Rose and Orpheus could feel Bronson's protective eye on them as the butlers slipped out the back door. Charlie Malone stayed at the rear. 'Bit of a lark, this,' he whispered.

This section of the city was gaslit, and they all carried lanterns. It was chilly outside, and droplets of rain fell. The wind ruffled Rose's cloak.

They walked down Riversgate, towards the Shudders. The Lord Mayor squared his shoulders. The alley looked cold, dank, dripping and uninviting.

'Be careful, sir,' muttered Miss Regemont. 'We will stay out of sight but close by. There may be other ruffians about tonight.'

'Like footpads or thieves,' said Bronson hopefully, her hand resting on her rapier.

The butlers positioned themselves at different points along the Shudders. Rose and Orpheus stayed with Bronson. Rose pulled her cloak around her shoulders, waiting. Every small noise unnerved her. The wind swept rubbish down the Shudders, and they heard distant laughter and singing from taverns.

The Lord Mayor set off down Mad Meg Lane. He walked out of sight. There was no sound. No cry, no footsteps. The place seemed deserted.

They waited for him to return. The time stretched out horribly.

'Probably a hoax,' Miss Regemont muttered. 'Anyone could have done it for a joke. Even the Wakemen might have been involved, as an act of revenge.'

'It could be an ambush,' said Charlie Malone. He looked around the dark streets. 'We should have thought of that.'

Brisk footsteps sounded. Everyone jumped, then pretended they hadn't. The Mayor had returned, looking rather disappointed.

'So much for that,' he complained. 'No sign of anyone. A hoax after all.'

Then they heard a growl.

The Lord Mayor spun on his heel. They peered into the skitterway. Their lanterns barely pierced the dark. But they did see a figure in the dark, something moving. Rose caught her breath.

With a muffled oath, the Lord Mayor drew his pistol and fired.

Someone shrieked in the skitterway. Orpheus lifted his lantern. A pale face showed in its gleam.

It was Miss Wildcliffe.

'What on earth?' sputtered the mayor.

'For pity's sake, you could have killed me!' Miss Wildcliffe came forward, holding a hand to her bleeding arm.

'What are you doing here?' demanded the

mayor. He looked very pale and his voice shook. 'Are you badly hurt?'

'I came to find out the truth behind the attacks,' said Miss Wildcliffe, her teeth clenched in pain. 'I received an anonymous note that said if I came here at midnight, I'd discover the real villain. I hardly expected to be shot!'

Everyone held up their lanterns, revealing the bloodstain spreading on her sleeve. Miss Regemont stepped forward and examined it as best she could. 'You were lucky,' she pronounced. 'I think the bullet only grazed you. But you need medical attention.'

She helped Miss Wildcliffe out of the skitterway. Charlie lit a candle from his pocket. Bronson took out her medical kit and began attending the injury.

The Lord Mayor was trembling. He dropped his pistol.

'Jane! You foolish girl! I've been trying to turn all those stupid rumours away from you – and you show up in the very place where the attacks occurred! Are you mad?'

'I'm sorry, Father,' muttered Miss Wildcliffe. 'But I wanted to help. The villain nearly killed you.'

'"Father"?' said Rose in amazement. 'Wait – Miss Wildcliffe is your daughter, Sir Edward? But you never said! Miss Wildcliffe never told us!'

'We have had our differences,' said the mayor gruffly. 'My last living child, and she despises me. Says my railways are ruining the countryside.'

'Well, they are!' snapped his daughter. 'It's shameful.'

'But you're not a Chesney. Your name is Wildcliffe,' Rose said, turning to the authoress.

'It's my pen-name,' Miss Wildcliffe explained. 'I don't like people knowing I am related to the Duke of the Railways.'

'How could you come out here alone, and risk being killed?' demanded the Lord Mayor.

'I wasn't by myself!' Miss Wildcliffe pointed.

'Constable Murton came with me – I asked him to, after I received the note. I wanted to help discover the truth behind these attacks.'

The policeman himself stepped out of the shadows. He stared at Miss Wildcliffe. 'She's alive? Not mortally wounded?'

'No, no, she will survive,' said Miss Regemont.

Rose watched the policeman closely. He didn't look relieved. He looked angry.

Rose stared at him. 'Oh,' she breathed in understanding. 'Constable Murton. You wanted Miss Wildcliffe to be shot.'

'Miss Raventhorpe!' exclaimed Miss Regemont. 'What a thing to say! Why on earth would he do that?'

'Revenge,' said Rose, softly. 'I read an article at Batty Annie's about the train crash the mayor was in. A woman and her baby died – they were a policeman's family, the article said. Constable Murton – that was your family, wasn't it? Baby Katie and her mother were killed in the crash.

That's why you hate Mayor Chesney. What better way to make him suffer than to have him kill his own daughter?'

There was a shocked silence. The constable said nothing in denial. He kept staring at Miss Wildcliffe.

'Surely it's not true,' said Miss Regemont incredulously. 'It can't be that this entire charade about the Barghest was a ploy to harm the Lord Mayor.'

'It was Murton who growled,' said Miss Wildcliffe. 'I heard him behind me.'

The constable swayed on his feet. He closed his eyes. 'My wife died,' he said. 'And our baby daughter.'

'Oh God,' whispered the mayor.

'You should have died instead of them,' cried Murton, in a flash of rage. 'The Duke of the Railways! Ha! You're a murderer, Mayor Chesney. Your railway killed my family.'

'But what about your other victims?' cried the

mayor. 'The pickpocket Moll? The girl Sylvia? They did nothing to you!'

'I didn't want to kill the pickpocket,' said Murton, with a sudden note of regret. 'That was a mistake. I only meant to hurt her, scare her. To start rumours against Miss Wildcliffe and her dog. But she fought back and I had to silence her. And I didn't kill that girl from the chocolate shop. She came roaring out at me – I only knocked her out.'

'But you still killed Moll the Pocket,' said Bronson coldly. 'You committed murder, and it was no accident like a train crash. Why go to all that trouble? Just to create fear and confusion?'

'I wanted people to blame the Moorland Witch,' said Murton, jerking his chin towards Miss Wildcliffe. 'She's always had funny rumours going about her, with her books about the Barghest. The stories were easy to spread. The placard, the pawprint – so simple to do. And it got under your skin, didn't it, Mr Chesney? Because your daughter was under suspicion. You thought she might be stoned in the street, the way things were going. So you got the Wakemen to plant that dead dog, didn't you?' He laughed mirthlessly. 'You were desperate, all right. Desperate enough to get your butler to help you, to find a dead mongrel and pretend it was the killer. Didn't work for long though, did it?'

'I tried to make reparation after the train accident,' said the mayor numbly. 'That's why I was in the skitterway that night . . .'

'Aye,' said the police officer. 'You were giving handouts to people that'd been in the crash. You sent your butler Rawlings to do it at first, but after the attacks you went out yourself.'

'So Rawlings was visiting accident victims when Moll the Pocket robbed him,' Rose said. 'That's why he was out late.'

'Yes, he was. A discreet man, Rawlings,' confirmed the mayor. 'He knew I didn't want publicity for those visits.'

'But the eyes,' said Orpheus. 'What about the red eyes?'

Rose looked thoughtfully at Murton. 'There was a theft at the Medical School recently,' she said. 'Chemicals were stolen. Was that your doing?'

Murton swallowed. 'What would I do with chemicals?'

'Please empty out your pockets,' said Bronson.

The constable did not move. Heddsworth stepped forward and patted the man's clothing. He drew out a clawed tool with sharp, curving metal prongs. Heddsworth held it with revulsion. Then he found a small bottle of white, crystalline powder.

'Let me see that.' Rose took the little bottle and opened her lantern. She dropped a pinch of powder on to the flame. The flame flared red.

'What is it?' she asked Murton.

The constable smiled.

'Strontium chloride,' he said. 'A chemical they

use in fireworks to make them red. I burned pine cones in a lantern to make red flames.'

'I can see why it scared people in the dead of night,' said Orpheus. 'How did you manage to carry it and attack people? Were you working alone?'

'I carried it at first,' said Murton. 'Low enough for a dog. Kept growling. That usually broke their nerve. Then I hid the lantern behind a step or a crate, and – I clubbed them down, and scratched them. I left the lantern after I killed the pickpocket – I had to run; there were people coming.'

'I saw the lantern,' said Rose, remembering. 'But no one was suspicious of you. Nobody would question a policeman being in the area. It was the perfect cover.'

'We should have asked the sweeps about the red fire,' said Bronson. 'They know how to make fireworks.'

'So it was all a trick,' said Miss Wildcliffe, as

Charlie bandaged her arm. She looked at the policeman. 'I liked you – and you were capable of all this!'

'For pity's sake, Murton, you would have received compensation money!' the Lord Mayor blurted out.

'I didn't want money! Money won't bring my wife and daughter back!' Constable Murton had a sob in his voice. 'What use is money? The law always goes soft on the likes of you.'

The mayor sighed. 'I am deeply sorry for your lost family, sir. But this is a poor sort of revenge.'

'How did you know Miss Wildcliffe was the mayor's daughter?' Rose asked suddenly.

'I found out when I was making a report on pickpockets to the Lord Mayor,' said Murton. 'I saw a painting leaning with its face to the wall and I was curious. I turned it over to have a look and saw Miss Wildcliffe was in it.'

'I turned that picture to the wall for a reason,' said the Lord Mayor fiercely. 'I lost my wife, my son and two of my daughters to illness. My other daughter would not speak to me. I could not bear to look on it. Do you think I don't know grief, young man?'

'I haven't anyone left!' cried Murton bitterly.

A police whistle rang in their ears. Sergeant Snodgrass appeared. He took in the scene before him with astonishment.

'I heard reports of a shot being fired,' he said slowly. 'I thought it was a hoax but it appears not.'

'Ah, Snodgrass,' said Miss Regemont. 'I am afraid your promising young officer has a confession to make. Have you anything else to tell us, Constable Murton?'

Murton sighed, and eyed Miss Wildcliffe's bandaged arm.

'I am sorry, Miss Wildcliffe. But I still wish Mayor Chesney had been a better shot.'

Chapter 16

A Vision in the Dark

Miss Wildcliffe was glad to return home to Withering Downs.

'I don't want to live with Father,' she told Rose and Orpheus, as they sat in her kitchen. 'Not yet. I don't want to live in Yorke. All that terror, created by one man's grief.' She paused. 'I hope this will make Father pay more attention to how he runs his train empire.'

'He does care about you,' said Rose. 'You are all he has left.'

Miss Wildcliffe sighed. 'Yes,' she said. 'I should visit him more often. And invite him to Withering Downs. He doesn't approve of my life here. But he is trying to do good, in his own way.'

'Is that what the stones told you?' asked Rose. 'The runes?'

'I can work plenty of things out without the runes,' said Miss Wildcliffe.

'At least the Barghest rumours will die down now,' said Orpheus. 'And innocent people like you won't be blamed.'

'Or my dog,' said Miss Wildcliffe, as Wolf slobbered over his bone. 'And no more butlers. Peace at last!' The butlers had left that morning for Silvercrest Hall, after many profuse thanks to their hostess.

'You were so kind, letting them stay,' said Rose.

'It was downright exhausting,' said Miss Wildcliffe.

'Here now,' said another voice. 'No mess in the kitchen, dog.'

Gowkins the farmer came bustling in carrying a tea tray. But he was no longer attired in farm clothes. He wore pinstriped trousers, a long tailcoat, white gloves, and polished black shoes. Miss Wildcliffe looked resigned.

'Gowkins!' cried Rose. 'You're becoming a butler?'

The young man nodded. 'I know I've a lot to learn, Miss Raventhorpe. And me dad wasn't over-pleased. But it's a grand job, mindin' a house. Miss Regemont said I could come to Yorke every week and take lessons, so I'd be a proper butler.'

'Are you going to learn to fence?' Rose asked, trying to imagine Gowkins with a sword.

'I'd probably cut somebody's ear off,' said Gowkins cheerfully. 'Not the best idea. Miss Wildcliffe's good with a pistol; she can defend the house from burglars.'

'It seems I cannot get away from butlers,' said Miss Wildcliffe.

Orpheus tasted one of Gowkins' scones. He winced. 'Ah, these are quite, er, chewy.'

'He's still working on scones,' said Miss Wildcliffe. 'But the pig will appreciate them.' She held out a book. 'Would you two like a new copy of my upcoming book, *The Spectre of the Skitterways*?'

'How lovely!' said Rose, secretly feeling that she didn't want to encounter spectral hounds ever again.

She and Orpheus left Withering Downs with extra scones pressed on them by Gowkins. Rose had lent the Raventhorpe carriage to the more elderly butlers so they could go home in comfort, and Gowkins insisted on giving the children a lift in the wagon, drawn by the ancient donkey. It took a long time to reach the city gates. Gowkins offered to escort them home, but the sky was heavy with storm clouds and Rose begged him to return to the moors before he was soaked by rain.

'I should have brought an umbrella,' said Rose, looking up at the sky. Lightning flickered from lowering clouds.

They hurried through the northern city gates and had just reached the Shudders when four or five butlers appeared. They all held lanterns and pieces of paper.

'Miss Raventhorpe!' called one. He bowed formally.

'Hello,' said Rose. 'Er – what are you doing?'

'We are having an international butlers' competition.'

'A what?'

'A race. So far the Scottish and the Japanese teams are in the lead,' put in another butler. 'We are the Swedish team. We are racing through the Stairs Below, and then we return to the Hall to take part in serving scones and naming teas while blindfolded. Tomorrow's event is shoe-polishing.'

'Oh,' said Rose. 'I see. Good luck.'

Off the butlers went. Rose giggled.

'I wish they'd told us,' said Orpheus. 'I would have taken part. I'm going to be a brilliant butler. The royal family will want me.' He shivered in the drizzle. 'Let me hail you a hansom cab home.'

'That's all right,' said Rose. 'You go along back to the Hall – I'll be fine.'

'Well – all right,' said Orpheus. 'You know the city better than most. I hope Heddsworth is on the mend. Shall we visit him again tomorrow? We can buy him some chocolates at the Emporium.'

'Yes! We have to tell him all about solving the murder.'

Orpheus disappeared into the dusk.

Rose passed Mad Meg Lane. Then she stopped. She would visit it once more. Just to see that people had grown reasonable again. No more scrawled warnings on the walls.

She walked into the alleyway.

It was deserted. The wind blew bits of paper down the cobblestones. Thunder rumbled in the distance.

Watchful the cat leapt over a rooftop. She felt relieved to see him. 'And where have you been?' she scolded him affectionately.

The cat paid her no attention. His attention was fixed on a shadow on the wall.

A large, slow-moving shadow.

Coldness crept down Rose's back. The shadow felt dark, ancient and malicious. It was too big for an ordinary dog, yet it was dog-like in its aspect. Two eyeballs flickered scarlet.

It was padding towards her.

Rose could not move. She was powerless against the evil that emanated from the creature. It snarled, a sound that reverberated through her body. It would leap at her, devour her, and leave nothing but dust in its wake.

Then Watchful landed on the cobblestones.

He looked puny compared to the shadow. But his own eyes flared golden, and he hissed. More cats, formerly statues on rooftops, came to join him, surrounding the shadow creature.

The hound – the creature – growled. The sound hurt Rose's ears. Watchful came to Rose's side. Drained of strength, she crouched and put her arms around him.

The shadow ran forward . . .

And for a moment, a brief flash of time, Watchful turned to stone.

Rose had a peculiar idea that she had too.

The cats hissed. Beyond the skitterway, in the wall of Yorke, a hole appeared. *A throughway*, thought Rose dazedly. A creep-hole. An escape.

The hound howled. Rose shut her eyes. It was a terrible noise, shaking the ground. The howl burned her, searing through her flesh. She put her hands over her ears, unable to endure it.

Strangely, with her eyes closed she could see images of animals. The cat statues, come to life. A raven. A hawk like Dauntless. Wolf, the fierce dog of the moors. They shrieked and growled and swiped with their claws. They menaced the shadow-creature, forcing it back. Towards the wall. Into the hole.

The hound howled once more.

Then it was gone.

Rose came back to herself.

She was alone in the skitterway. Watchful slunk around her legs. The other cats had disappeared. She gazed at her fingers, feeling their warmth.

She was halfway down the Shudders before she stopped shaking. People passed by her, absorbed in their business. Nobody looked bothered or anxious. With the arrest of the supposed Barghest, the panic was just another folk tale.

The next day Rose and Orpheus visited the Chocolate Emporium to buy a present for Heddsworth. Rose said nothing to Orpheus about her ordeal the night before – in the bright light of day she was beginning to think she had dreamed it.

The shop looked delicious. Its windows were packed with treats. Cakes of solid chocolate were decked with chocolate-coated cherries.

Multi-coloured sweets glittered in crystal jars. Inside, the room was warm and full of customers. Lorimer was almost run off his feet, packing bags and boxes of chocolate, and ringing up sales on the till. He smiled at Rose over a bouquet of toffee flowers. 'Miss Raventhorpe! And Master Orpheus! Are you both well? Would you like some chocolate?'

'Yes, please,' said Orpheus. 'I mean, if you insist.'

'How is Sylvia?' Rose wanted to know.

'Recovering, miss,' said Lorimer happily. 'Dr Jankers is looking after her. He has agreed that she should give up the confectionery trade in favour of studying in the medical school.'

'Good for her!' cheered Rose.

Lorimer presented them with a massive basket of treats. They thanked him and carried it between them down the street.

Orpheus paused. 'Oh, look – Batty Annie!'

The elderly Junkyard Queen shuffled into view. She held a bouquet of buttercups. 'Ah, the Raventhorpe girl and the sailor's boy,' she said. Her stare seemed to sink into Rose. 'You saw off the beast,' she said. 'The Barghest has left the city – his presence is gone. I thank you for that. My niece can rest in peace now.'

'Thank you,' said Rose. She saw Orpheus's puzzled expression and hastily added, 'I'm glad we discovered who committed the murder.'

Batty Annie smiled knowingly. 'The walls are safer now. Can you not feel it?'

'Yes,' said Rose. And it was true. She had returned to the Yorke walls that morning. Her heavy feeling of dread and wrongness was gone, blown away like a cloud. She wondered if Batty Annie knew Rose had once suspected her of murder.

Batty Annie nodded in a satisfied way, and went off towards the skitterway, to lay her bright bouquet at the site of her niece's death.

'Maybe we should take the Stairs Below,' she told Orpheus. 'It'll be faster.'

'All right,' said Orpheus. 'The door off Cornsgate is nearby.'

By unspoken consent they did not take a shortcut through a skitterway. They walked down the Shudders and made their way to the quieter street of Cornsgate. Feigning interest in the shops, they waited until nobody was looking their way before Rose took her Infinity Key from its locket and opened a door in a wall.

They lit a lantern and set off with the basket of chocolates. The scent was mouthwatering.

'I hope this doesn't attract rats,' said Orpheus wickedly.

'Ugh!' said Rose. 'Let's hurry.'

They kept walking, the light of the lantern bouncing ahead of them.

'Someone else is in here,' said Orpheus suddenly, his voice low. 'There's another light.'

Rose saw it too. She thought of the International Butlers' Brigade. 'Maybe they're having another day of racing instead of shoe-polishing,' she suggested.

'We'd better keep out of their way then.'

This section of the Stairs Below was narrow.

Rose hoped the butlers would have room to pass. The footsteps that approached sounded unsteady. A lone competitor. Rose held up the lantern.

A wild-eyed, grimy apparition came into view. He was breathing harshly.

Bathory.

Rose gasped. She and Orpheus dropped the basket and drew their rapiers.

'What are you doing here?' Rose whispered. 'How have you been living here all this time?'

'There's water,' said Bathory. 'The walls are damp in places. Pools. Puddles.' His hungry gaze fixed on the basket, with its pile of sweets.

'You've been hiding in the Stairs Below?' said Orpheus. 'But you didn't know they existed!'

'I found these secret tunnels of yours while I was in the Hall,' said Bathory. 'Got through that door when you lot attacked. Thought they had to come out somewhere, but there's nothing but locked doors!'

'You must have used almost all the lanterns,' said Orpheus, staring at the weakly flickering light.

'Almost,' said Bathory, still grinning. He pushed a lank lock of hair out of his eye. 'So you'll be left in the dark. Should be fun, if I leave you alive.'

'We'll let you out,' said Rose. 'We'll let you go – I have the key.'

'Put your little toys down.' Bathory took a pistol from his pocket. 'I've got two shots left.'

'Bullets will ricochet in here,' warned Orpheus.

Bathory laughed, and cocked the pistol. 'Throw your swords away and I'll think about it.'

They had no choice – Bathory looked mad enough to attack. Very reluctantly, Rose and Orpheus dropped their blades behind them.

'No butlers or cats to look after you in here,' said Bathory. 'Which one of you wants to die first?'

A noise behind Bathory startled them all. It sounded like pebbles falling.

'Blasted rats,' said Bathory. 'I've been skewering them down here. They taste terrible.'

Rose regretted dropping her rapier. She would rush Bathory, she thought. He was weakened by starvation. If she could get the pistol away from him, they might survive this encounter. She tensed herself to spring.

Then another figure stepped out of the gloom behind Bathory and a sudden flash of silver sent the pistol flying into a muddy puddle.

Heddsworth moved into the lantern-light.

'Enough of threatening children, Bathory,' he said. 'If you want to fight, I will take up the challenge.' He drew a black glove from his pocket and threw it to Bathory. It was the butlers' invitation to a duel.

Bathory glanced scornfully at the glove. 'Oh, you would do it like that. Aren't you tired of rescuing these two?'

'Are you all right, Heddsworth?' stammered Rose. She was horribly frightened for Heddsworth – she'd had no idea he had been released from hospital. If Bathory dared to hurt Heddsworth again she would fight him herself, armed with nothing but chocolates and rat droppings.

'I am mending,' said Heddsworth. He looked pale, but he was dressed in his usual butler attire.

Bathory snorted. 'I take it this is a duel by blade?'

'If you don't mind,' said Heddsworth. 'You're weak and so am I. We should be evenly matched.'

'Suitably dramatic, I suppose.' Bathory drew his rapier. 'Do tell me, is this to the death?'

'I would prefer to avoid that outcome, regardless of who wins.'

'We'll see,' said Bathory. 'There's no room here for fancy tricks.'

Rose and Orpheus drew back, rapiers at the ready should Bathory try to run. The combatants lifted their blades. Rose held her breath.

There was a strange, deadly casualness about their first strikes. Bathory looked almost bored. Heddsworth was on the defensive, letting Bathory attack.

Then Rose noticed something. Heddsworth was

fighting with Sigandus. He had not had his rapier in the hospital, and this was his only weapon.

The ancient blade could not be easy to wield, especially in the narrow confines of the Stairs Below. Rose had felt the weight of that blade. It was hard work for Heddsworth, who was perspiring. In the flash of light from a lantern, Bathory noticed the blade too.

'The sword,' he hissed. 'So you did have it after all! Well, I'll take it as a keepsake once I'm done with you.'

Bathory dashed forward, trying to run Heddsworth through. Heddsworth barely managed to block him with Sigandus.

'It's no sword for a butler!' sneered Bathory. 'Its powers are for true fighters!'

Heddsworth rallied. His eyes were blue fire.

'Only butlers and their friends may use this sword,' he responded. 'And you would make a *terrible* butler.'

With a flash of Sigandus, the paw-shaped brooch

on Bathory's cloak went flying. The Wakeman tried to swipe at Heddsworth's legs. Sigandus blocked him. The ancient sword gleamed silver in the lantern-light.

'I can carry full tea trays up stairways without spilling a drop,' said Heddsworth, parrying with Sigandus. 'I can slice cucumbers paper thin with my eyes closed. I can polish silver until it blinds you, but what most needs polishing here is *your manners.*'

And he brought the full force of Sigandus down on Bathory's rapier. The rapier snapped in half like a toothpick. Bathory stared at his broken weapon in disbelief. Then, with a howl, he threw it away and sank to the ground.

'You're all right?' Rose asked Heddsworth anxiously, darting forward. 'You're well again?'

'Indeed I am, Miss Raventhorpe,' said Heddsworth as his eyes met hers. 'Let's just say I found a throughway in the wall.'

*

Rose, Orpheus and Heddsworth escorted Bathory out of the Stairs Below and into the Yorke police headquarters. Sergeant Snodgrass was delighted to arrest him for attempted murder.

'Thought you could run our city, eh?' he growled. 'You took over that Hall, overruled the police force, and tried to make this place your own? Splendid – you will be right at home in Yorke Prison.'

They returned to Silvercrest Hall to find the butlers putting the final touches to the restoration of the Hall and they all jumped in to help. Inaaya dusted chandelier crystals. Orpheus cleaned silver, while Rose folded napkins into fans and Miss Regemont ordered about the younger butlers in training. 'The velvet drapes must be brushed and the china cleaned. Is the door to the Stairs Below in good repair?'

'All is well now, madam,' said Heddsworth, coming in. 'We only need the crest back. *Et gladio et polies.*'

'Oh!' said Rose. 'I'm sorry, I used it as a shield in the battle with the Wakemen. It got a bit dented.'

Heddsworth picked up the crest from the round table. He ran a gloved finger over the dent. 'Excellent,' he said. 'We shall leave it as it is.' And he went to replace it on the door.

Rose saw then that Sigandus had been set over the door in a pair of brackets.

'Perfect,' exclaimed Rose. 'But don't you want to put it in a display case?'

'I believe we should keep it where we can use it, if needed,' said Heddsworth. 'What do you think?'

Rose remembered what Batty Annie had said about the sword. That it would protect a person from the Barghest. That it could cut a hole in walls. And she remembered that shadow moving towards her, and the eyes glowing in the darkness. The cats and their allies coming to her defence. If it hadn't been for them . . .

'I think it's a good idea to keep it,' she said, repressing a shiver. 'Just in case.'

LETTERS FROM EMILY

Dearest Rose,

Thank you so much for agreeing to be godmother to little Werther and Charlotte! Our darling twins will benefit greatly from your care. I assure you it will get easier to change diapers. I find it a delightful challenge. And Spillwell is excellent at giving them bottles.

Miss Jane Wildcliffe has agreed to be a godmother. She sent them rattles carved out of oak, from a tree that grew over a poet's grave. The perfect present.

The twins adore Bertram the Second, and pull

his tail. Dearest Harry is already teaching them magic tricks. You can teach them languages, and how to solve mysteries.

Love,

Emily

Dear Rose,

I invited Miss Wildcliffe to our latest Poetry and Parasols soiree, and she actually came! Can you believe it? I was enraptured! She brought her new butler, Gowkins, with her. What a sweet man he is. It is not every butler who can run a household AND deliver piglets. I am sure he has a poetic soul, living out on the moors and being so devoted to Miss Wildcliffe. He even contributed his own poem. I have included it here:

There was a fog on Withering Downs
So misty, cold and damp
It froze the mud in every bog
And made me fingers cramp.
A dreadful rattlin' filled the air
And shook the fastened doors
A beastie crept into the room
On hulkin' muddy paws!
It was the evil Barghest

A tremendous hound of woe
It opened its enormous jaws
And met a mighty foe.
T'was a Heroic Butler
In his boots and polished hat
Who hurled a teapot at the beast
Just like a cricket bat!
The beast did howl and turn his tail
And evermore shall flee
For woe betide the deadly hound
Who interrupts High Tea.

Rose, it is a WORK OF GREAT GENIUS. I asked Miss Wildcliffe for her opinion but she declined to comment. It caused a sensation at the soiree. He was in great demand afterwards, but insisted on pouring the tea, rather than signing autographs.

Incidentally, Miss Wildcliffe brought her dog Wolf with her. Wolf tried to steal Bertram's bone, and Bertram actually nipped him on the nose. I don't think Wolf has ever been challenged in his life. He and Bertram had a big noisy fight, but now seem to be best of friends. I had no idea that Bertram had such courage. It is lucky he was never mistaken for the Barghest!

Your dear friend,

Emily (Patroness of Yorke Poets)

Dear Rose,

I am glad you liked the poem! I agree, it is quite remarkable. And how sweet of Orpheus to commit it to memory and quote it to you so often!

By the way, Harry and I have agreed with Dr Jankers and Lorimer to advertise their new chocolate company on our hot-air balloon. 'The Yorke Chocolate Emporium' has a splendid ring to it. Besides, we get a selection of free chocolates and sweets every week. The twins will adore it once they are old enough to eat them. Harry suggested throwing out free sweets over the city from the balloon, but I fear from a certain height they may become dangerous missiles.

We visited the shop the other day, and it was delightful. We even saw Miss Wildcliffe buying chocolate. She was with her father, the mayor. They seem to be getting on better now, despite a good many arguments about nature and railways.

Lorimer has made special christening biscuits for us with the twins' names iced on them.

We gave some chocolate to Batty Annie, the fortune teller. She said, 'The sword must rest where it now lies'. How enigmatic and romantic! I asked her what she saw in the future for my children. She said they would acquire a taste for literature. Isn't that marvellous?

Must go, the twins are chewing on my copy of Miss Wildcliffe's book.

All my love,

Emily

Glossary and Fun Facts

Barghest: A Barghest is an eerie, spectral dog that is supposed to prey on lone travellers in York's snickelways. There are many versions of supernatural dogs in British folklore, including the Gytrash, Skriker, and Church Grim. Most are fearsome, but some are regarded as guardians. Sir Arthur Conan Doyle drew on such legends when he wrote the Sherlock Holmes story *The Hound of the Baskervilles.*

Chocolate: York has a tradition of chocolate-making. In the eighteenth century, names like Rowntree's and Terry's became famous and gave

York a new economic lease of life. Many famous chocolate bars originated in York. Today, the city celebrates this part of its history with tourist attractions like chocolate-themed shops and factory tours.

Sword of State: The city of York really does have a Sword of State. It's called the Sigismund Sword, and has been used in civic ceremonies since the 1400s. The original was given to the city by King Richard II, when he went to York to avoid the plague in London. The original sword did go missing, and had to be replaced. I've made up my own version of what happened to it.

Wakemen: The name 'Wakeman' comes from an ancient tradition in Ripon, Yorkshire. A wakeman, or hornblower, was a night watchman who blew a horn each night to indicate he was on the watch. This practice started a thousand years ago and is still going strong. The original horn, the

Charter Horn, still exists in Ripon. One legend has it that the former Lord Mayor, Hugh Ripley, will appear and disasters will occur if the horn is not properly sounded.

York Minster Police: York Minster has its own police force, the only cathedral in the world to do so. However, they are not called Wakemen. As far as I'm aware, they are very nice people and have never behaved like the ones in my story!

The Duke of the Railways: My character Sir Edward Chesney is inspired by George Hudson, the 'Railway King' of York. Hudson made a fortune in railways and became Lord Mayor, but lost his reputation due to unscrupulous business practices. He died a relatively poor man.

Cat statues: There really are cat statues on buildings in York. Most have been put up quite recently, but they were inspired by much older versions. Legend has it they were meant to scare off vermin from the city.

Skitterways: I called the little alleyways and snickets in the city of Yorke skitterways. I thought this sounded like the skittering of alley cats, ducking from place to place. A twentieth-century author, Mark W. Jones, gave the alleys in York the wonderful name of 'snickelways'. Sadly for me, this name didn't exist in the Victorian era.

Acknowledgements

When you're dealing with scary deadlines, spooky first drafts and eerie amounts of editing, it helps to have brave and brilliant people on your side. I'm extremely lucky to have my agent Polly Nolan and my editor Lena McCauley. Their tact, skill and encouragement should be rewarded with riches and an endless supply of chocolate. I also thank Lisa Horton for her stunning cover design, and all the lovely people at Little, Brown and Hachette.